Righting a Wrong

Righting a Wrong

Rachael Anderson

HEA Publishing

ISBN 13: 978-1-941363-02-7
ISBN 10: 1941363024

Published by HEA Publishing

The Ripple Effect Romance Series

*Like a pebble tossed into calm water,
a simple act can ripple outward
and have a far-reaching effect on those we meet
perhaps setting a life on a different course—
one filled with excitement, adventure,
and sometimes even love.*

Other Works by Rachael Anderson

Novels

The Reluctant Bachelorette (A *USA Today* bestseller)
Working it Out
Minor Adjustments
Luck of the Draw
Divinely Designed

Novellas

Twist of Fate
(found in the *All I Want* anthology)
The Meltdown Match
(found in *A Timeless Romance Anthology: Summer Wedding
Collection*)

For my beautiful and talented niece, Cambri.
You're as gorgeous on the inside
as you are on the outside.

Prologue

Late November

Thick snowflakes dotted Jace Sutton's windshield, slowly marring his view of the rundown bungalow-style house with a for sale sign pounded into the frozen ground out front. He eyed the home with a mixture of irony and resignation. In two weeks, he'd officially be homeless, and unless he wanted to move in with his grandfather and sister—which he didn't—Jace needed to make an offer on a house soon.

Only ten months earlier, his best friend had swooped into town, turned the head of Jace's girlfriend, Eden, and stolen her heart. Now Drew wanted to steal Jace's house too. Well, not *steal* exactly, more like take back what rightfully belonged to Eden. It was the house she'd been raised in, the house where her roots were firmly planted, the house she would always call home. The only reason Jace had purchased it from her in the first place was because she desperately needed the money and wouldn't accept his help any other way.

So Jace had moved in, and Eden and her mother had moved out. Jace had fixed up a few things here and there, including replacing the warped and damaged hardwood floors. But instead of installing the rich mahogany planks he'd always wanted, he went with a knotty light oak color because it was the closest match to the original floor. He'd wanted to knock down walls, open up the living space, and replace the cobblestone fireplace with white painted wood paneling and a large, craftsman style mantle. He wanted to update the kitchen cabinets, the bathroom tile, and the freestanding vintage bathtub that Eden's grandmother had picked out herself.

But if he did any of that, he'd be changing a place that was dear to Eden's heart, and he could never bring himself to do it. He'd loved her that much, even though it was never enough for either of them. So when Drew came knocking on his door, asking to buy it back for his new wife, Jace had agreed. And although it was difficult to see them so happy when he was left alone, it was better this way. The house was finally back in the right hands, and Jace could now get the fresh start he needed.

Unfortunately for him, there were only three homes on the market in Bridger, Colorado. And since Jace didn't know what to do with ten acres of farmland or have the money to repair a cracked foundation and some major structural damage, that left only one option—the home currently disappearing behind the soft layer of snow on his windshield.

There was no denying it had character or that enough sweat equity could turn it into something he'd always wanted. The fact that it was close to the store and situated in a quaint neighborhood was an added bonus. Really, nothing should stop him from snatching it up and thanking his lucky stars it was available—nothing except the painful memories it unlocked every time Jace looked at it. Maybe he was cursed or just plain unlucky because it seemed to be his lot in life to own yet another home that held a special place in the heart of a woman he'd once loved.

But where buying Eden's home had felt like a step in the right direction, contemplating the purchase of this house felt like a huge step backward, reminding him of a girl he'd rather forget.

But what other choice did he have?

He drew in a deep breath as the house disappeared completely. Maybe this was a good thing. Maybe, if Jace got to work covering up the old with the new and took a chainsaw to that cursed maple tree, he might finally be able to erase the memory of a certain girl who'd once wanted to buy this house and make it her own. A girl who'd gotten in the way of every relationship he'd ever had.

One

Early Spring, Five Months Later

Cambri rolled down her car window and breathed in the fresh air. It had been nearly six years since she'd navigated these streets—not that there was much to navigate. The town consisted of one stoplight, a handful of stop signs, and a lot of intersections with no signage at all. There was a time when Cambri had thought it was the perfect size, but after living in University Park, Pennsylvania and Charlotte, North Carolina, she'd come to realize that Bridger was as podunk as they came.

She turned down her old street and unconsciously slowed the rental car she was driving. A few trees had grown larger. A few homes had obviously gotten a new paint job. A yard that was once fenced was now open, and a yard that was once open was now fenced. But overall, her street remained unchanged.

And then she saw the home where she'd grown up.

Cambri pulled to a stop, and her mouth went dry. *What happened?* Where was the large pine and the aspen trees, or

4

her mother's favorite rose bush that had once softened the far side of the front porch? Where were all those colorful irises that would have been standing alert, ready to bloom any day now? It looked as though someone had gone through the yard and plucked out all the beautiful flowers and shrubs so weeds like purslane and morning glory could have free rein. Even the grass was riddled with crabgrass and dandelions.

The yard had once been her mother's pride and joy, and now—now it was gone.

Dad! What have you done?

Cambri left her suitcase in the truck and headed for the house, unable to look at the yard any longer. It wasn't until she'd raised her hand to pound on the door that she hesitated. Was she ready to face what was on the other side? Was she ready to see her father again?

No. She'd probably never be ready, but she couldn't put it off any longer either. With a deep intake of breath, Cambri forced her hand forward and knocked, then cringed at how hollow and empty it sounded, as though the house were only a shell of its former self.

Footsteps were heard before the door creaked open, revealing Suzie Small's sweet, elderly face—a neighbor who had lived across the street for as long as Cambri could remember. Her hair had thinned, and a few more wrinkles covered her face, but Suzie's smile was the same as it had always been—warm and sincere, like a large bear hug.

"Cambri Blaine, is that really you? Come in and let me have a look at you!" Her gnarled and fragile hands came to rest on Cambri's cheeks. "Your face is a breath of fresh air, my dear. We've missed you so."

"Speak for yourself!" snapped a deep voice from the back. "I told you I don't need a babysitter, especially someone who has no interest in me. I can take care of myself."

Suzie rolled her eyes before giving Cambri a light pat on the cheek. "That's his way of saying he's missed you too," she said quietly.

Yeah, missed me the way a fish misses a hook in his gut, Cambri thought dryly, then gave Suzie a quick hug. "Thanks for calling me and for looking out for him until I could get here."

"It was no trouble. No trouble at all." Suzie picked up her purse from the sofa table and slung it over her petite shoulder. "They only discharged him this morning, so he's in need of a few groceries. I didn't want to leave him, but now that you're here, I'm going to run and pick up a few things and let you two catch up. But I want to hear about all your adventures when I get back, you hear?"

Cambri nodded. "Thank you, Suzie. For everything."

The door closed behind her, and an almost eerie silence engulfed the house. The blinds were closed, making it feel dark and stuffy. And the smell—wow. The house could definitely use an airing out. But at least the inside didn't look as though it had been stripped and left forgotten like the outside. The piano was still in the living room next to the old floral couch, and all the family pictures still hung on the wall.

The old hardwood floor creaked as Cambri walked toward the kitchen. She dropped her purse on the counter before making her way toward her father's darkened room. He lay in his bed, looking thinner and older than a nearly seventy-year-old body should look. His bald head had wrinkled with age, and the lines around his eyes and mouth had deepened. A heavy feeling filled Cambri's chest. It shouldn't have taken six years to return.

"Hey, Dad."

Without looking her way, he said, "I told you I don't need a sitter. I'm not some feeble, sick person."

Cambri cocked her head to the side. "You had a heart attack. I'm pretty sure that makes you at least a little feeble for now."

6

A grunt sounded, and her father folded his arms the way a small child would do when throwing a tantrum. Cambri almost smiled. Almost. The reminder that she'd nearly lost her one remaining parent kept it away.

She would have gripped his aging hand in hers, but her father would have none of that. Harvey Blaine didn't believe in sympathy. To him, it was a sign of weakness, and he was anything but weak. The fact that he'd survived a massive heart attack attested to it. According to doctors, it was a miracle he was still alive.

Now it was Cambri's turn to perform a miracle by getting her stubborn father to take his meds, rest, get to his appointments on time, and adjust his high-cholesterol diet to something rich in vitamins, fiber, and heart-healthy protein. With his arms still folded and a slight pout on his lips, Cambri had her work cut out for her.

A recliner sat in the corner, and Cambri plopped down on it, tucking her legs under her.

"What about your job?" her father said. "Don't they need you there?"

Cambri shrugged. "I had some vacation time coming, and my boss agreed to let me do some work from here and telecommute on the days he needs me. Looks like I'm all yours for a few weeks."

His mouth fell open. "A few weeks! What willy-nilly doctor told you I'd need anyone for that long? Give me a day or two, and I'll be back on my feet."

"Let's wait and see what the doctor says at your next appointment. Until then, you're going to get plenty of rest, take your medicine, and eat whatever I make for you."

"I don't see how that will help—unless your cooking's improved since high school. I'll probably starve."

Cambri sighed. This was going to be a long few weeks. She mustered a perky tone and changed the subject. "What's happened since I left?"

Breathing heavily, her father flopped back against his pillow. "Catching you up on six years will take longer than a few weeks, that's for sure. Maybe if you'd called once in a while, you wouldn't be so ignorant."

Cambri refused to let him get to her. It wasn't as though he'd picked up the phone either. "Other than Suzie, who's still around? The Clements?"

Her father nodded.

"Engersolls?"

Another nod.

"Whitakers?"

He huffed. "Good riddance."

"Suttons?" Cambri kept her tone flippant, but she listened hard for his answer.

"As if Cal would ever leave. He's too loyal for that—not that you know what that means."

Cambri disregarded the gibe. "What about Mr. and Mrs. Sutton? They still around?"

He huffed again. "They took off not long after you."

It was on the tip of Cambri's tongue to ask about Jace, but she bit back the question. If his parents were no longer around, chances were that he wasn't either, especially since Jace used to have his sights set on bigger things than Bridger. Which was a good thing. As difficult as it was to face her father, bumping into Jace would have been ten times worse.

"Speaking of the Suttons, do you still fish with Grandpa Cal?" Cambri asked, reverting to the name she used to call Jace's grandfather years earlier. Her father had been forty-three when Cambri was born, making him about the same age as Jace's grandfather. The two had always been great friends, though Cambri had never figured out why. Grandpa Cal was all warm fuzzies whereas her father was a prickly pear.

"He's not your grandpa. And yes, I do—when I'm not in the hospital or in bed."

His comment hit a tender spot, and a lump formed in Cambri's throat. What if he hadn't made it? What if she was here for a funeral instead of caring for him? She needed to remember that when he started getting under her skin, which he would.

Cambri rose from the chair and paused with her hand on the doorjamb. "Is there anything special you'd like me to make for dinner?"

"Aren't you going to kill the fatted calf?" he said sarcastically.

"Haha." But the barb hit its mark. Cambri knew before she came that she wouldn't get the best reception, but she'd hoped for a *little* more warmth. For most people, a close call with death would make them grateful for what they had. But not so with her father. If anything, he was more of a curmudgeon than ever.

Cambri left the darkened room behind and walked straight to the nearest window, where she lifted the blinds and opened it. Sunlight and fresh, early spring air drifted in, lifting her spirits.

She could do this. She could get through these next few weeks, whip her father's body back into shape, and return to her peaceful and happy life in Charlotte.

Two

"Morning, Dad." Cambri walked around his bed and twisted open the blinds, allowing warm rays of the morning sun to stream into the room. "Sleep well?"

"What in tarnation are you doing?" he spluttered. "If I'd wanted those shades open, I would have done it myself."

Cambri ignored his comment. She'd spent several hours the night before talking to Suzie and reading all the literature her father's doctor had sent home, and one of the things she'd learned was that heart attack survivors were prone to depression during the weeks following the attack. Harvey Blaine had always been surly, but Cambri wasn't about to let him become depressed as well. Sunlight was a natural mood lifter, and she would make sure he got plenty of it.

She moved to his nightstand and opened one pill bottle after another, collecting his daily dose. Then she held out a glass of water, along with the handful of pills. "Breakfast is almost ready. If you take these, I'll bring it in."

Her father eyed her hand with disdain. "I feel fine. I don't need a bunch of medication to mess that all up."

"No medication, no breakfast." Cambri wriggled her palm.

"What's for breakfast?"

Her eyebrow lifted. "I can tell you it's not the fatted calf."

Although he harrumphed, a twinkle of humor appeared. "I almost forgot how cheeky you could be."

"And I almost forgot how ornery you could be."

He rolled his eyes but grudgingly accepted the pills, swallowing them with a sip of water. Then he settled back against his pillow. "I always have sausage, eggs, and hash browns on Saturdays."

"Believe it or not, I remember." Cambri retrieved a breakfast tray from the kitchen and set it on his lap, mentally preparing herself for what would come.

"What's that supposed to be?" Her father stared at the food in disgust.

"Oatmeal, whole wheat toast, and freshly squeezed OJ," said Cambri smoothly. "Try it. You might like it."

"Why isn't there butter on this toast? Where's my sausage and hash browns?"

"Your heart doesn't want bacon and hash browns. It wants oatmeal."

"Bullwinkle."

Cambri had to bite back a smile at that. When she was a little girl, her father used to cuss at everything. One day, she'd repeated some of those words, and her calm, quiet, and usually sweet mother totally lost it. She told Harvey that if he didn't stop cussing right then and there, she'd move back to Denver and live with her mother.

From that moment on, Harvey adopted a new method of cursing. He started using expressions like thunderation, son of a biscuit, or shiitake mushrooms—all of which earned him a chuckle rather than the evil eye from Cambri's mom.

And now here he was, with his wife nearly nine years gone, still using her preferred method of cussing.

Moisture pooled at the base of Cambri's eyes, and she had to blink it away. Emotion made her father uncomfortable, and she wasn't about to let hers show. She drifted to the window where the overrun yard lay beyond.

She cleared her throat. "I was thinking I'd clean up your yard a little today, but I can't find any of Mom's old gardening tools. Do you know where they are?"

"I gave them away." He continued to glare at the oatmeal as though it should know better than to show up on his breakfast tray.

"You *what?*"

"I hate yard work. Always have. Why would I keep a bunch of tools lying around that I don't use?"

Cambri refrained from pointing out that he obviously didn't hate yard work that much if he took the time to pull out all of her mother's old plants, but she swallowed the retort, knowing it would only lead to an argument.

"I guess I'm headed to the hardware store then. Need anything while I'm out?" The doctor said he didn't need constant supervision, and Cambri had no qualms about running a few errands. If she never got a break from him, he'd be in more danger of death by strangulation than a repeat heart attack.

"If I said a burger and fries, would you bring it to me?"

"No."

"Then no," he muttered.

"Enjoy your oatmeal," Cambri said brightly before collecting her purse and walking out the door, where she inhaled the fresh, clean air that smelled of vegetation. In Charlotte, the air always seemed to be tinged with carbon monoxide and too many people living in close proximity to each other. It felt good to be back, and she realized with a start that she'd missed this place.

Familiar houses passed in and out of her peripheral vision as she drove, and before long, she pulled to a stop in front of Sutton's Hardware—a place where she used to hang out often. For a moment, she allowed her heart to ache with a sense of loss, but then she squared her shoulders and left the car behind, ready to prove that she'd moved on with her life.

With confidence, she walked inside and breathed in the familiar smell of tools and lumber. She smiled at the woman behind the cash register, glanced at a display of home improvement magazines, and headed for the gardening area, only to be sidetracked by the small greenhouse attached to the side of the store.

Cambri walked into the small room and wandered up the aisle, looking at the plants. The selection was poor, and the quality even poorer. For the most part, the leaves were turning brown around the edges, looking so thirsty and pitiful that Cambri had to do something about it. Spying a hose with a sprinkler attachment not far away, Cambri turned it on and began spraying everything. When the pots were filled to overflowing, she grabbed a pair of the smallest sized pruning shears she could find that weren't packaged in plastic. They were much larger than she needed, but they'd do the job.

Starting with the worst of the plants, she clipped away, trimming the dying limbs with the hope of inspiring new, healthy growth.

"What are you doing?" a deep voice said from behind her.

Cambri finished trimming the plant then turned around. "Just saving your—" The words died on her lips as she stared into the dark brown eyes of Jace Sutton. At least she was pretty sure it was him. Gone were his glasses, his lanky body, and the way he'd avoid eye contact at all costs. He stood tall, his shoulders wide, his bearing confident. His

13

dark hair was no longer parted on one side and swept to the other. Instead it was styled in that disheveled, carefree way. The pruning shears dropped to her side as she stared.

Clark Kent had become Superman.

Three

In Cambri's life, mistakes were like boomerangs. She'd make them, regret them, and launch them as hard and far as she could to get away from them. Then suddenly, after she thought they were long gone, they would come sailing back to thunk her hard on the chest.

Like now.

Cambri could practically hear the figurative boomerang whooshing toward her as recognition dawned on Jace's face—the kind of recognition that came when seeing someone from your past you'd rather not see.

"Hey, Jace," was all she could come up with to say. She clutched the pruning shears, frantically trying to think of something more. "Long time no see."

He glanced at the shears, and a few awkward seconds passed before he responded. "Yeah, long time."

"I was just, uh . . ." Cambri brushed a few dried leaves off the shears and held them up. "Trying these out. They're sharper than I expected. I'll take them."

"Will you take the hose too, or was it the sprinkler head you were also *trying out*?"

Cambri gave up the pretense. "They needed water, okay? These plants are dying."

"How nice of you to care about their welfare."

"I'm a landscape architect now. Plants are sort of my thing."

He nodded slowly, watching her with a face as poker as they came. "I'm glad to hear that. It's what you always wanted to do."

"Yeah." No longer able to meet his gaze, Cambri set down the shears. "What about you? Did you ever get that construction management degree?"

"I own the store now, so I guess you could say tools and lumber are my thing."

That didn't answer her question, but she got the impression he didn't really want to answer it. "Oh. I didn't know that."

"There's a lot of things you don't know."

Yeah, got that. First from my dad, and now from you. Cambri should have grabbed the first trowel she found and ignored the pitiful plants. She could have been long gone by now.

"How's Harvey?" Jace asked.

"Good." Cambri said. "And by good, I mean he's hanging in there. Still as surly as ever though. You know him." Probably a lot better than she did. The thought was a humbling one.

"We're all glad he's okay." Jace's gaze moved past Cambri and out the window, as though searching for any excuse to get away from her.

Like the plants behind her, Cambri wilted a little, although she wasn't sure why. Running into him was bound to be awkward and uncomfortable. She knew that. So why did his cold reception sting so much? "Yeah, me too."

He searched her face once more, as though trying to read beyond her words and into her thoughts. As the seconds ticked by and the air between them thickened with a tense silence, he finally took a step back and directed his thumb over his shoulder. "Rebecca's working the counter. She can ring you up."

"Thanks."

He nodded. "I've got to run. I'm late for . . . a meeting." He spun around and left, leaving Cambri to watch him walk away. With every step he took, Cambri's heart sank a little more. Almost without thinking, her fingers pressed lightly against her lips as the memory of an unexpected yet searing kiss teased her senses, followed by the aching throb of regret.

From the day they'd been matched up as partners in their junior high biology class, Jace had been her best friend. It had been an unlikely friendship—the confident, popular girl and the awkward, nerdy kid—but Jace had surprised her. He became the person she could talk to about anything and everything, the person who made her laugh when she was down or helped her think about things with a new perspective. When her mother had died, and her father buried his pain under his typical gruff exterior, Jace had been there, offering his shoulder for her to cry on, just like any really good friend would.

Cambri had thought they were both clear on the definition of their relationship, but as it turned out, he'd held something back—a game changer. One kiss their senior year in high school and everything stable in Cambri's life shifted. Everything safe became scary. And the one person she thought she knew better than anyone else suddenly wanted more than she was ready to give.

But she shouldn't have left the way she had, with things between them so unfinished and exposed. As her best friend, Jace had deserved some sort of explanation, at the very least a phone call. But every time Cambri picked up her phone, she realized she had no idea how to explain.

In the end, she'd managed to ruin the best friendship

she'd ever had.

Yeah, big thunk. Probably the worst one yet.

But if there was one thing Cambri had learned how to do over the years, it was to chuck that boomerang once more, harder and farther than the last time, then run sideways to avoid ever seeing it again. Sometimes, when it came to boomerangs and mistakes, the only thing you could do was exercise avoidance maneuvers.

From here on out, all gardening tools would be purchased in Fort Collins.

Jace tapped the hammer against the edge of the last wood plank of his new mahogany floors. He'd cut it a tad too long, but after making one mistake after another all night long, he was going to make this piece fit if it was the last thing he did. He drove the hammer down harder, and the plank dug into the drywall at the base of the wall. One more slam, and it finally went down, trapping enough drywall beneath it to keep it propped up slightly.

Jace cursed—something he rarely did. Then he pried it back up, pushed broken and powdery drywall to the edge of the wall, and slammed the plank down again. It landed flush this time, and the light caught the mild imprint of a hammer head on the end. No matter, that would get covered up by the baseboard.

"Finally." Jace stood and brushed his hands together. He would have been finished hours ago if he'd been able to focus. But thoughts of Cambri had plagued him ever since he'd bumped into her at the store, looking so good he could hardly pry his gaze away. Her hair was longer and darker, as though she'd colored it, and she looked older, more sophisticated, and, well—citified. But her eyes were still that bright green he'd always loved, and the mole on her cheek near her upper lip still twitched when she didn't know what to say.

Jace frowned. Why had she been there anyway? She'd looked as surprised and panicked to see him as he was to see her, but what did she expect? It was Sutton's Hardware, for crying out loud.

Jace kicked at one of the several discarded planks. So much for having enough flooring left over for the half bath. A few of these could be reused, but that was it. He'd either have to order another box or lay tile instead.

Things had been going so well. The weather had been fairly decent throughout half of February and most of March, and Jace had been able to get the exterior almost done, giving the house a new, non-reminiscent-of-Cambri look. The inside had been coming along too—until now.

A knock sounded at the door, and Jace called out. "It's open!"

Drew popped his head in, then walked inside. He looked over the floor. "Wow, this looks great. I'm impressed."

"Thanks," said Jace. "What's up?"

He held up a pot of something. "You know Eden. Always worried about other people and whether or not they're eating enough. She knows how hard you've been working, so she made you some soup."

It was typical Eden—something she'd done often for him when they were dating and every so often once he'd started work on this house. But whenever Drew showed up with something in hand, Jace wondered how much was out of kindness and how much was out of guilt—not that she had anything to feel guilty for. Eden fell in love with someone else, and that was that.

"Be sure to thank her for me," said Jace.

Drew dodged all the scrap planks as he made his way to the kitchen. "Looks like you've got a lot left over. Enough for the half bath like you'd hoped?"

"Maybe, if I wouldn't have made so many mistakes."

"Whatever," Drew joked. "You're Jace Sutton. You don't make mistakes."

Jace gave him a look that said *yeah, right.*

"Need any help?"

"Thanks, but no. I'm going to call it quits tonight. With the way I'm mixing measurements up, I'd ruin a bunch of trim as well."

Drew leaned against the counter. "Something on your mind?"

There was a time when Jace might have talked to Drew, but these days he preferred to keep his problems to himself. "Just an off day."

Drew nodded, looking as though he didn't believe him, but at least he'd learned not to prod for more.

"How's Eden?" Jace probably shouldn't have asked because he didn't really want to know. But after all Drew and Eden had done for him to try to keep things from being awkward, Jace could at least pretend like they weren't.

"Good. I mean, school keeps her pretty busy, but she's loving her classes. And we get to see each other at Silver Linings, so that's definitely a plus. Things are . . . really good."

"Good." Although Jace knew things were better than good. He'd run into the two of them around town enough to know that they were beyond happy together. Eden practically glowed, and Drew looked like he'd just won the lottery. Jace wanted to be thrilled for them, but the hollow, emptiness inside always took over, turning his good wishes into words that sounded flat and contrived.

"You sure you don't need any help?" Drew asked. "I can help clean up if nothing else."

"No. You get back to Eden. I'm good here."

"Okay." Drew pushed away from the counter. "Guess I'll leave you to it then."

"Thanks again."

"No problem."

The door closed behind Drew, and the sound echoed through the empty house like a cruel reminder of Jace's current relationship status. There was a time when Jace was sure he'd found *the one*, but unlike Drew and Eden, his and Cambri's connection had only been one-sided. And now she was back in town, digging up old feelings and memories that were best left buried.

Jace grabbed a spoon from the drawer, sat on the counter, and ate Eden's homemade chicken noodle soup. The warmth acted as a calming agent, restoring some much needed inner peace.

Cambri wouldn't be in town forever. As long as Jace could stay out of her way until she left, he could get back to moving on with his life without interruption.

Four

"Son of a bucket!" Cambri's father's voice boomed from his bedroom.

She sighed, staring at a landscape plan that she'd promised to get to her boss by the end of the week. Unfortunately, her father was making it difficult to keep that promise. It had been three days since she'd arrived in Bridger, and every time she sat down in front of her laptop, her father seemed to need her for something. A drink of water. Couldn't find the remote. Would she get the mail or drop something by the post office?

For someone who swore up and down he didn't need a sitter, he was certainly making use of her.

Cambri left her laptop on the desk, shut her blinds to the darkening sky, and went to discover what her father was up to now. She found him sitting at the kitchen table, rifling through a bunch of fishing stuff, searching for something.

"What are you doing, Dad?" Cambri asked, picking up one of his flies to examine. It was black and yellow, looking like a small, fuzzy caterpillar. Interesting.

"I can't find the new carbon hooks I just bought," her father muttered. "I know I put them in here." He lifted his box, as though intending to turn it upside down and spill the remaining contents all over.

"Wait." Cambri rested her hand on his to stop him from making an even bigger mess, then pulled out a package of fishing hooks from the kitchen junk drawer. "You mean these hooks? I found them on top of the fridge when I was cleaning yesterday."

Harvey frowned at the hooks, then at Cambri. "If you think I'm losing my marbles, you're wrong. My mind's still as sharp as a tack. Suzie must have taken them out of my box and put them there."

"I'm sure she did," Cambri said dryly. As though Suzie would ever do something like that.

"She likes getting under my skin." He held out his hand. "Now give 'em here. I'm already running late."

Cambri had started to hand over the hooks, only to take them back. "Late for what?"

"Fly tying at Cal's," he said as though Cambri should have already known that. "We do it every other Tuesday."

Her fingers tightened around the package of hooks, keeping them secure in her hand. "Correction. You did it every other Tuesday *before* your heart attack. Now you're taking one or two weeks off."

"Poppycock. I can sit at Cal's house just as easy as I can sit here."

Did her father really think she would just let him walk out the door that easily? "You're not allowed to drive yet, remember?"

"You can drive me."

Cambri shook her head. "Sorry, I've got work to do."

"Then I'll walk." He started packing up his box as though he intended to do just that.

"Go ahead and try," said Cambri. "You can't even walk from one side of the house to the other without getting winded. You'll never make it."

"What did I do to deserve a daughter like you? No loyalty whatsoever." Harvey shook his head as though disgusted with her. "Guess I'll just have to call Jace to come and get me."

Wait—Jace? Come here? The mere mention of his name caused a pit to form in Cambri's stomach. "Okay, you win. I'll take you."

One of his eyebrows lifted. "Thought you had work to do."

"I'll drop you off and come back here." Now that she thought about it, this could actually be a good thing. With her father at Grandpa Cal's, the house would be quiet and peaceful. Suddenly anxious to get him out the door, Cambri scooped up a handful of fishing stuff and threw it in the box.

"What in flying French fried hogs are you doing? Those don't go there."

Cambri leveled him a look that said she'd had enough. "You said you were running late."

He huffed in response, but didn't say anything else as they finished cleaning up.

As Cambri pulled out of the driveway, her father said, "Head north on Main then take a left on Silver."

"I remember where Grandpa Cal lives." Just because Cambri had been gone for a few years didn't mean she'd forgotten Bridger or the people who lived here. But instead of heading toward Main like her father suggested, Cambri took the back roads. Whether it was because she didn't like being told what to do or because she suddenly felt like taking a jaunt down memory lane, she wasn't sure. Maybe it was a little of both.

When she took a left on Rose Street, she immediately felt a rush of nostalgia. This had always been her favorite street in all of Bridger. The houses were close to each other, but not too close, the trees tall and shady in the summer, and the overall ambience oozed character and charm. The fact that her mother's name had been Rose only made her love it that much more. There was one house in particular that she'd always dreamed of owning.

Cambri slowed the car as she approached the two-story bungalow home, then stopped and stared. It was no longer white, but a steel blue with white trim around the windows and newly painted pillars around the huge front porch. And the large maple—Cambri's favorite tree in all of Bridger— was gone. And fairly recently too from the looks of that large hole where its massive trunk had once sat.

"Aw," Cambri said, unable to keep the slight complaint contained.

"Something the matter?" Her father's voice cut through her thoughts, bringing attention to the fact that Cambri was being ridiculous. This wasn't her house. This wasn't her town. That wasn't her tree. Why did she care? She leased a beautiful condo back in North Carolina and had nearly enough saved to buy her own.

"Nothing's wrong," she said. "I've just always loved that house. I'm sad to see the maple tree gone." Just like she'd been sad to see her father's yard all torn up. Her heart ached with a loss she couldn't quite explain.

"Interesting," said her father.

Cambri glanced his way, noting an amused gleam in his eyes. "Why is that interesting?"

He shrugged. "No reason. Just find it . . . interesting."

Knowing she'd get no further explanation than that, Cambri left the home behind and drove the rest of the way to Grandpa Cal's place, which looked exactly the same as it had years earlier. *Bless you, Grandpa Cal.* The only difference was an older, charcoal-gray Tundra in the driveway.

Cambri stayed in the car, waiting for her father to get out.

Her father paused with his finger on the handle. "You're not coming in?"

"I told you I was just going to drop you off, remember? I've got a bunch of work to get done. Call me when you're done, and I'll come get you."

"Don't you at least want to say hi to *Grandpa* Cal?" asked her father, emphasizing the word Grandpa.

Cambri shot him a my-patience-is-wearing-thin look and unbuckled her seatbelt. But it would be fun to see Grandpa Cal again, and a couple of minutes wouldn't hurt. She grabbed her father's tackle box and followed him to the front door, where he gave three hard raps. A moment later, the door opened, and Jace's handsome face appeared.

Cambri nearly dropped the tackle box.

"Harvey, what are you doing here? We didn't think we'd see you for at least—" The words abruptly ended when Jace caught sight of Cambri standing in the shadows behind her father.

"Hey again," she said, feeling stupid and awkward. Why hadn't her father mentioned that Jace would be here? Cambri would never have agreed to come inside, not even to see Grandpa Cal. She took a step back. "Well, Dad, it looks like you're in good hands. What time will you be done? I'll come back to pick you up then."

Her father looked at her like she'd grown two heads. "Thought you wanted to say hi to Cal. And Jace is here. Don't you want to catch up with him too?"

"Oh," Jace inserted. "We already, uh—caught up at the store the other day."

Harvey looked from Cambri to Jace and back to Cambri. "If you two have already *caught up*, why does it feel like we're all standin' on a bunch of eggshells?"

Cambri wished she had one of her Mom's old hankies so she could shove it in her father's mouth to keep him quiet. "I have no idea what he's talking about. Do you, Jace?"

"Nope."

"Great, then lead the way to Grandpa Cal. I'd love to say hello really quick."

26

Her father nodded in satisfaction and headed inside, pushing his way past Jace. "I'm sure he's downstairs."

Jace continued to hold the door open for Cambri as well. She caught a whiff of something sporty and woodsy and had to catch herself from leaning in and sniffing. He smelled so familiar, like a scent reminiscent of a really fond memory.

"What are you doing here?" she said, trying to ignore the way his close proximity brought on a severe case of the butterflies. "I thought you hated fishing—especially fly fishing."

"I do," he said.

Cambri waited for more, but it didn't come. "Oh, sorry. The way you answered the door made it sound like you're a regular to these, uh . . . bi-weekly meeting things, or whatever they call them."

"Fly tying nights," Jace said, closing the door. "And I'm here to prevent injuries."

Cambri raised an eyebrow, and Jace sighed as though he was being forced to carry on a conversation he had no desire to carry on. "After spending two different nights in the ER getting fish hooks out of thumbs, I figured it would be less time-consuming and expensive to oversee the tying."

She winced as she pictured her father with a hook in his thumb. "I'm surprised they let you take them to the ER."

"I didn't give them a choice," said Jace. "I told them it was either that, or I'd admit them to Silver Linings and wash my hands of them both."

Cambri laughed. "I wish I could have been a fly on the wall for that conversation. I bet the look on Dad's face was priceless."

"He did call me a cotton-picking lint licker or something like that." Jace smiled slightly, and the corners of his eyes crinkled.

Cambri couldn't resist reaching out to touch him just to the side of his right eye. "You're getting wrinkles," she teased.

She'd meant to lighten the mood with the gesture, but the smile slipped from his face and a strange sort of energy filled the space between them. He studied her for a few seconds before taking a step back and breaking the connection.

"Grandpa's downstairs," he said.

Cambri's hand fell to her side. She watched him trot down the stairs, admiring his athletic grace and wondering where the awkward teenager had gone. When he glanced back and caught her looking, she mentally berated herself and followed. The large family room at the base of the stairs looked the same as she remembered, only with several more fish mounted to the wall.

"Well, if it isn't Cambri Blaine!" a deep voice reverberated throughout the room.

Cambri looked over in time to see Cal Sutton's large arms open and engulf her. "How ya been, girl? We've missed you around here."

She soaked up the warmth of one of Grandpa Cal's bear hugs, realizing how much she'd missed this wonderful man. How come her own father couldn't greet her this way?

"Let me have a look at you." Cal's large hands framed her face, and his smiling eyes met hers. "You've grown into a lovely young woman," he said, grasping her left hand and raising it. For a second, she thought he meant to kiss it, but instead his eyes twinkled. "And still single too, I see."

Cambri gave a short laugh and pulled her hand free. "And you're still a tease."

He chortled and wrapped an arm around her shoulder, guiding her toward a large wooden desk in the corner. "It's been way too long. I need you to tell me all about school, your job, and the East Coast. I've always wondered what kind of fishing they have over yonder."

It occurred to Cambri that her father had never once asked about school or her job, but it was the first thing out of

Grandpa Cal's mouth. "School was great, and North Carolina is lush and green, with beautiful beaches. I love my job and am sorry to report that I know nothing about the fishing there, or fishing in general."

"Well, you're in luck." Cal clapped his hands together and rubbed them. "Tonight you're going to learn something about fishing that not many people know. Have a seat."

"Oh, you're sweet to offer, but I can't stay. I've got work to do."

"She keeps saying that," her father muttered.

"Cambri, sweetie." Cal pulled out a chair for her. "It's been way too long since you've been in my house, and I'm not about to let you hug and run. Surely your work can wait a few minutes," he pleaded, and Cambri knew she couldn't say no.

"Okay, but just for a few minutes."

Grandpa Sutton smiled, then pulled a chair next to hers and began teaching her the art of tying flies. Using a small vice to hold the hook, he wrapped floss around the feathery stuff, securing it to the hook, and within minutes, he made a cute little fuzzy creation called a dry fly hackle.

Cambri quirked an eyebrow at Jace. "I'm not understanding how a hook got caught in anyone's thumb. That vice holds it amazingly well."

"One of the incidents happened before the vice."

"Before? But how can you tie one of these without—"

"Exactly," Jace cracked a smile. "Harvey wanted to save the money and insisted he could hold the hook just as well as any vice could."

Cambri laughed. "How did that work out for you, Dad?"

A frowning Harvey continued his search for the perfect piece of hackle, as though he hadn't heard her.

"And the second incident?" Cambri asked.

The chair creaked as Jace leaned and put his hands behind his head. "That one happened when they tried to remove the hook from the vice for the first time. Gramps didn't loosen it enough, and it ended up in his thumb."

Cal nudged Cambri with his shoulder. "I was just testing the vice to see how strong it really was. Turned out we got a good one." His eyes crinkled like it was a hilarious inside joke.

"I'm just glad you finally figured it out so there won't be any more trips to the ER," said Cambri, shooting a glance at Jace. "Which leads me to wonder why you still come if they really don't need you anymore."

He shrugged. "I think it's pretty interesting and have nothing better to do, so I keep coming."

Harvey's hand landed on Jace's shoulder, and he gave him a prideful shake. "We all know you have plenty to do. You're here because you're a good, loyal grandson, and that's that."

Loyal. There it was again—the only trait her father seemed to care about, which also happened to be a trait he thought his daughter lacked.

Cambri slid a hook into the vice and started tightening it. "Mind if I try one, Grandpa Cal?"

"Have at it."

It took a few failed attempts and some coaxing on Cal's part, but Cambri finally figured out how to get the floss started. As she cut a piece of hackle and removed some strands near the stem, she peeked at Jace, her curiosity getting the better of her. "What brought you back here? I thought you were headed to college for a construction management degree because you wanted to start a development company."

Jace's jaw tightened at the question. "Plans change sometimes."

Harvey grunted. "I'll tell you what changed. After Cal retired, Jace's parents decided to move to a warmer climate, and since Cal had already retired and didn't want the

30

business anymore, Jace came back to keep them from selling." He directed a meaningful look Cambri's way. "Like I said, loyal."

"No." Jace shifted in his seat, looking uncomfortable with the compliment. "Being away at school made me appreciate home. I wanted to come back."

Cambri returned her attention to the fly. Her father could make all the snide comments he wanted about her leaving, and although they stung, Cambri had always been able to shake them off. Tons of people moved away from home to pursue their dreams—people who were considered brave and independent, not disloyal. But after hearing Jace's story and what he gave up for his family, Cambri couldn't help but wonder if she was the person her father made her out to be.

Things might be different if she'd found a way to leave on good terms. Or if she'd stayed in touch with more than the expected birthday or Christmas call. Or if it hadn't taken six years and a heart attack to get her to visit.

Her stomach clenched, making her feel queasy and uncomfortable. With quick, almost jerky movements, she wrapped the floss around the hook, securing the hackle to it in an imperfect way. Her few minutes were up. She was ready to leave.

Cal caught her hand, slowing her down. "Easy does it. Remember, you're making a fly, not mummifying it." His words were spoken in a light-hearted way, but they still opened the floodgates on Cambri's emotions. The moment tears started to threaten, she handed Cal the bobbin, stood, and made for the stairs.

"I'm sorry, but I've really got to go," she said, hoping no one heard the slight catch in her voice.

Footsteps sounded behind her on the stairs, and she quickened her steps.

"Cambri, wait." It was Jace.

She paused with her hand resting on the front doorknob, wanting to fling it open and run away, but some unseen force kept her rooted with her back to him.

"Is something wrong?"

Cambri swallowed and tried to keep her voice steady when she answered. "I'm fine. I just need to get some work done."

"Oh." He paused. "Don't worry about coming back for your dad. I'll make sure he gets home okay."

Of course he would, because Jace was loyal, just like her father had said. It made Cambri both hate him and admire him at the same time.

"Thanks," she said. Then she twisted the knob, slipped through the door, and walked as quickly as she could to her car. If there was one thing she was a pro at doing, it was running away.

Five

After her run-in with Jace at Grandpa Cal's, Cambri doubled her efforts to avoid Jace, but it didn't help. Everywhere she went, she bumped into him. At the grocery store, bank, even while she was stopped at the one traffic light in town. He'd crossed the street in front of her and had even nodded her way.

Stupid, small towns.

But at least one thing was looking up. An entire week came and went with no major run-ins with her father. Although he still grumbled about taking his meds and eating healthier meals, he was becoming a much better patient, for which Cambri was grateful. She even managed to get a little work done.

"What are you doing?" she asked her father when she found him opening drawer after drawer in the kitchen.

"Where are my keys? The zoning meeting starts in fifteen minutes."

Which was exactly why Cambri had taken preemptive measures to hide said keys at the bottom of her underwear drawer. Her father would never look for them there.

"No idea," she lied easily.

He leveled her a look. "You hid them, didn't you?"

"I plead the fifth."

He planted both palms on the counter and narrowed his sparse, gray eyebrows. "Cambri," he warned.

He was breathing heavily, as though the exertion of searching for keys had exhausted him. She sighed and pulled out a barstool for him, then took a seat on the one next to it. "You're not allowed to drive, and I don't want you going to that meeting."

"Why the blazes not? How hard is it to plant my tush in a chair and observe?"

Cambri leaned against the counter and folded her arms. "You know as well as I do that you don't plan to plant your tush in your chair and observe. I overheard you talking to Grandpa Cal, and I know you're against the rezoning. If I let you go, you're going to be on your feet the entire time, shouting your version of obscenities at anyone who crosses you. Admit it."

He frowned and leaned more heavily on his hands. "I'll stay seated and keep my trap shut."

"You couldn't do that even if you wanted to, which you don't."

"Fudgecicles!"

Cambri eyed his trembling hands, wishing he'd take a seat right now. "I guess we're at a stalemate then. I can't force you to stay, but you can't force me to give you the keys either. If you want to go, you'll have to walk." They both knew he could never make forty feet, let alone the three miles.

Harvey stiffened and lifted his chin. "I'll call Jace. He'll come get me. Or better yet, you call him. He's the type of solid, down-to-earth guy you should set your sights on. Not some eastern city boy."

Something cracked inside Cambri, and her jaw tightened. "If he's so good, why would you want to saddle him with me? How's that fair?"

"What are you talking about?" Her father finally gave up his power-stance and dropped down on the nearest bar stool, taking large gulps of air.

"All you've ever done is talk about how great Jace is—how he's smart and loyal and going somewhere. But when it comes to me, all I've ever heard from you was that cheerleading was for girls without brains and landscape design was a wishy-washy career choice and I'm disloyal for wanting to pursue a life outside of Bridger. Never once have you said anything good or positive about me. You didn't even come to my college graduation—"

"Please," he huffed. "Flying is for people with a death wish. How did you expect me to get there?"

"A *loyal* father would have driven," she said, pointing out his hypocrisy. She shoved her chair back and stood, glaring at him. "I have a wonderful life and career now, and I've made something of myself. But heaven forbid you see it that way. Instead, you sit there and call me disloyal, when I've just uprooted my life to fly back here to help you."

His hand slapped the table. "You had choices. You could have gone to a closer school or taken a job in Denver. But instead you chose to move to the other side of the country, as far away as you could possibly get. Why?"

"Because it was the best school. Because Mom was gone. And because you've never given me a reason to feel any loyalty to you at all," Cambri blurted. She knew she'd gone too far, but his accusations had cut her deeply, and she couldn't rein in her temper. She'd had it with her father *and* with Bridger. If she could pack her bags and walk out the door right now, she would.

"I'm glad to hear that walking away from your family has made you happy."

Cambri threw up her hands. "Oh, for Pete's sake, Dad. What family? Mom was the glue that held us together, and after she died, you went your way, and I went mine. End of story."

"You mean *you* went yours. I stayed here." The words came out breathless and weak, as though it took a lot of effort to speak them.

Cambri took a deep breath and struggled for control. Getting her father to see things from her perspective would never happen, and all she was doing by arguing with him was endangering his heart and hurting hers. It was time to put an end to this conversation.

"Right," Cambri finally said, her voice quiet. "You stayed here. And as soon as you get back on your feet, you'll continue to stay here, whereas I'll go back to my life in North Carolina. In the meantime, let's try to get through these next few weeks without any more arguments, okay? This isn't good for your heart."

"And do what? Sit in silence for the rest of your visit? Where's the fun in that?"

Cambri gaped at him. He thought this was fun? Was he joking?

They both sat there, glaring at each other—an unspoken face-off. After a few moments, something sparked in her father's eyes—something that looked a bit like pride. "Well, I can see who you got your stubbornness from, and it sure wasn't your mama. She was as sweet and obliging as strawberry Jell-O."

The reminder of her mother's nature sent a sharp pang to Cambri's chest. If Mom was looking down on them right now, she wouldn't be happy. *Contention is of the devil*, she'd always said.

Ignoring her father, Cambri grabbed her purse from the counter and headed for the door. "If you'll be all right for a few hours, I'm going out."

"To do what?"

"To get away from you before I clobber you over the head with a rolling pin."

Her father made a low guttural sound. It took Cambri a moment to realize he was chuckling, and the sound made her stop short. How had they gone from yelling at each other to this? It didn't make sense—*he* didn't make sense. In her current mood, the last thing she wanted to do was laugh or get chummy with her dad. Maybe the heart attack had addled his brain as well.

"If you're going out, you might as well do something useful and go to the town meeting. You can tell me what happens."

As if. "I'm not a member of this community anymore."

"You can represent me," he continued. "Tell them I don't want no developer coming in and slapping up a bunch of houses like those patchwork quilts that Suzie makes."

Cambri spun around and molded her face into a smile as she backed toward the door. "You're right. I should go to that meeting."

Her father grinned. "That's a good girl. You do that. You tell them—"

"That Harvey Blaine is all for the zoning change. They can buy all the land they want and develop away."

Cambri continued to watch her father long enough to see his smile disappear, then her smile became genuine as she turned and walked out the door.

The room smelled musky and dank, and the walls were the color of bread dough. The meeting was already underway, so Cambri crept up the aisle and slid into the first vacant seat she found. Despite what she'd said to her father, she hadn't planned on coming to the meeting. But she'd forgotten that everyone came to these things, which meant everywhere else was closed. So unless she wanted to hang out in her car or walk aimlessly around Bridger during a chilly spring night, she had nowhere else to go.

A large hand landed on hers, giving it a quick squeeze. Cambri's gaze snapped to Cal Sutton's welcoming face. Beyond him, Jace met her gaze with an unreadable, almost wary expression.

Oh joy. Of course the first vacant seat would be right next to them.

Cambri focused her attention on the man speaking from a podium at the front of the room, who was in the process of introducing another man from a company called Callahan Development.

"Are you stalking me?" a hushed voice sounded at her side, making Cambri jump. Jace had leaned forward and was talking around his grandfather.

"No."

"Then why do I keep bumping into you everywhere I go?"

"Why would I be stalking you?" she whispered back. "I think you're stalking me."

"I was here first, just like I was at the grocery store and bank first, so how could I be stalking you?"

"Because you knew I'd be there—and here." It sounded ridiculous, but so was the idea of her intentionally seeking him out.

"Seriously?"

"And how convenient that the only aisle seat left just so happens to be right by you."

"Please." Jace smirked. "How would I know you'd be here? You don't live here anymore, so why in the world would you come to a town meeting?"

To get away from her father, not that he'd really know that. "Dad couldn't be here, so I came instead."

His expression became more serious. "You're planning to represent your dad?"

"Well no, not exactly. I'm actually thinking I might argue *for* the development." She said it to be cheeky, because if her father was against it, then it followed that the loyal Jace would be against too.

Jace's eyes sparkled with something resembling humor. "In that case, welcome." He settled back in his seat with a satisfied smile.

Cambri frowned in confusion. What was that supposed to mean? Was Jace actually *pro* the development? Did her father know that?

Huh.

Cambri nudged Cal. "So, what's your take on the new development?"

Cal shook his head in that vague way that implied he was keeping his opinion to himself. "I'm only here for moral support. Jace is the owner of the store now. This is his fight."

What did Sutton Hardware have to do with anything? Was Jace hoping the store would become a supplier? Because that was a long shot. Longer than long, actually. He'd never be able to match or beat the prices of the larger, more specialized companies.

It wasn't until the discussion was well underway that Cambri understood Jace's stance.

"It's not just the hardware store. All the businesses in town are struggling," Jace argued. "We could really use some growth here. More people means more business, which is a good thing for any town."

"But with growth comes more competition," someone else called out from the back row. "What would you do if Bridger grew so large that a Home Depot decided to come knocking on the door?"

Jace shrugged. "It would be a long time before that ever happened, and when and if it ever does, I'll deal with it then.

In the meantime, I'm trying to run a successful business *now*, and it's a tricky thing to do in a town as small as Bridger. Especially in this economy."

Jace looked Cambri's way, shooting her a challenging look. "Cambri Blaine is here to represent her father, and she agrees with me."

Whoa, what just happened? How dare he bring her into this? He knew she'd only been teasing before and had no opinion on the subject. But a lot of surprised eyes were now trained on her, expecting her to validate Jace's sketchy claim.

She shifted in her chair. "Actually, my father's against the development," she said, not wanting to lie.

Jace raised an eyebrow and prodded further. "What about you? You've lived in a larger city for a while. What are your thoughts on the subject?"

"I—uh . . ." Why was he putting her on the spot like this? Did she even have an opinion? If Cambri still lived here, if she owned her own landscape business, would she be on Jace's side, fighting for growth and progress? Would she be okay with Bridger growing and changing?

An image of Bridger with multiple traffic lights and congested streets came to mind, making her frown. The truth of the matter was that while she appreciated Charlotte and everything it had to offer, she loved the quiet hominess of Bridger and didn't want it to change.

"I'm going to have to side with my father on this one. I like Bridger the way it is," she said finally.

Murmuring broke out around the room, and Jace's expression fell slightly. But he regrouped and continued to argue his side, citing statistics and testimonials of citizens from other small towns who didn't let growth scare them away from progress. A few other people, including some store owners, joined in the fight, and coupled with the developer's presentation, they made a convincing argument. But in the end, not enough people owned struggling businesses and too many people were resistant to change. The petition for the zoning variance was voted down.

Cal heaved a sigh, patted Jace on the back, and moved to talk to someone, leaving Cambri alone with Jace. Her heart went out to him—the lone voice against a crowd of naysayers—but what could she do?

"I'm sorry, Jace," she said.

"Me too." He shoved his notes into the shoulder bag he'd brought with him and slung it over his shoulder. "I thought you, of all people, would be on my side."

She rested her hand on his arm, but when he tensed, she pulled it away. "University Park and Charlotte are beautiful cities with so much to offer, but Bridger isn't without its charms. Coming back here is like entering a different world."

"An archaic world."

"That's not what I'm talking about," said Cambri. "People here know and care about each other. When you walk down the street, you pass friends instead of strangers. The air is cleaner, the pace slower, and the world calmer. I'm pretty sure the sky is even bluer."

Jace slung his bag over her shoulder and leveled her a hard look. "Actions speak louder than words, Cambri. Or are you forgetting you left for *bluer* skies six years ago?"

Her gaze held steady. "Sometimes it takes seeing other skies to know which is bluer."

One eyebrow quirked as he considered her words. "What are you saying? That you've had your fill of city life and want to move back?"

Cambri looked away. *Was* she saying that? No, of course not. That would be crazy. She was happy in Charlotte. "All I'm saying is that I appreciate Bridger a lot more than I used to."

He let out a low chuckle that didn't sound even close to humorous. "Like I said, actions speak louder than words." He started to walk past her, then paused, looking beyond her to the back door. "You talk of passing friends instead of strangers, but in my experience, friends are really just strangers disguised as familiar faces." His arm brushed against her shoulder as he left, and an uncomfortable, almost palpable, sensation spread down her arm and landed with a thud in her gut.

A stranger, he'd called her. Someone he didn't know at all.

Why did that bother her so much? Cambri had spent the past six years trying to forget him and the past week doing her best to avoid him. His comment should feel like a well-deserved set-down, a slap on the wrist, a lesson learned the hard way. Not a sucker punch to the chest.

An unsettling realization struck her. She still cared about Jace's opinion. It wasn't working to ignore the past and hope it would go away. She needed to make things right—or, as right as she could make them. Jace had never gotten an explanation or even an apology, and as much as Cambri cringed at the thought of exposing a six-year-old wound, it was probably the only way to stop it from festering.

Maybe it was time to stop acting like a stranger and become a friend again.

Six

According to Murphy's law, toast will always land butter side down, if you're in a hurry, every light will turn red, and in Cambri's case, the moment she decided she wanted to bump into Jace was the exact moment it stopped happening.

She'd tried the hardware store first, followed by the grocery store, the post office, the eatery, the diner, the bank, and finally the hardware store again. But no Jace. Not even a sighting of Jace. He'd either fled town or donned an invisibility cloak because he didn't seem to be anywhere. And with every passing day, Cambri felt like her window of opportunity was becoming less of a window and more of a closed door.

Her foot tapped restlessly against the carpeted floor of the doctor's office. A magazine bounced in her lap, unread. It had been over forty-five minutes since her father had been called back to see the doctor, but it felt like two hours. She should have insisted she join her father despite his protests.

A tinny ringing sounded, and Cambri pulled her phone

from her purse, then sighed when she saw her boss's name. She accepted the call and put the phone to her ear.

"Hey, Dillon."

"Sorry to bug you, but I just got off the phone with Belinda."

"I'll have the plans to you by the end of the week," Cambri promised. *So long as I can get Jace off my mind and learn how to focus again.*

He chuckled. "I know you will, which is why I need to tell you that Belinda now wants a pool in that far corner instead of the secret garden. But she still wants the pool to have a secret garden-y feel, like a small pond."

"You're joking." The secret garden was the one thing Cambri had already finished. And it had turned out perfect, some of her best work yet. She cringed at the thought of clicking Delete.

Stupid, *stupid* Murphy's law.

"Are you really that surprised?" Dillon said. "You had to know that it was only a matter of time before her husband convinced her to go with the pool. He never wanted the garden."

"I know, but . . ." Belinda had been so adamant and her husband so willing to make his wife happy. And the secret garden design had been both challenging and fun.

"Tell you what," Dillon said. "Let's bump the deadline to Monday instead of Friday. I'll break the news to Belinda, and that will give you a few extra days to work on it."

"Thanks, that'd be great." Cambri ended the call with a heavy heart. She'd done enough pool designs that it wouldn't take long to make the change, but it bothered her that she found no excitement in the prospect. Usually she couldn't wait to get going on new projects.

Stupid, stupid Jace.

Maybe it was time to take matters into her own hands so she could stop stewing about it.

The door finally opened, and her father emerged with the doctor at his side. Since Murphy's law was hard at work on all the other aspects of her life, Cambri readied herself for some more bad news.

"Are you Cambri?" the doctor asked.

"Yes." She set down the magazine and stood, accepting his proffered hand.

He held out some packets of information, along with a few brochures. "I had a feeling that you'd never see these if I didn't give them to you personally."

"What are they?" Cambri said as she accepted them.

"I'd like your father to start exercising every day. He should have started last week." The doctor eyed Harvey with a disapproving glance. "But I get the impression he hasn't done much."

"I've been doing plenty," Harvey argued.

Cambri rolled her eyes. "If by 'much' you mean walk around the house and complain about me putting things where they don't belong, then yeah, he's done plenty."

The doctor chuckled. "Well, it's good to hear he's been up and about—not that I expected otherwise. But I'd like him to take a walk around the block every day and gradually build up the distance he's able to go. He needs to start getting his heart back in shape."

Cambri opened the pamphlet and looked over what appeared to be a recommended exercise schedule. She looked up. "Tell you what. I'll make sure he gets a daily walk in, if you remind him that he's not allowed to drive yet. He doesn't think I know what I'm talking about."

The doctor turned a weary eye on Harvey. "Stop giving your daughter a hard time, will you? You know you're still on too many meds for that to be safe. Feel free to get out and walk around your neighborhood though. Do as much as you can without over-taxing yourself."

"I'm not going out walking like some old geezer in a retirement comm—"

"Thanks, doctor," said Cambri, cutting her father off. "I'll be sure to see that he starts walking right away."

Her father grumbled, and the doctor nodded. "I'm glad you were able to come back for a visit. It sounds like you're exactly what your father needs."

Cambri nudged her father. "Hear that, Dad? I'm exactly what you need."

He harrumphed. Shocker.

Cambri steered him out the door, picked up a salad on the way home, watched him eat it, then coerced him outside. "It's a beautiful day," she said. "Let's go out and enjoy it."

"I told you, I'm not—"

"Dad, *please.*" Her tone must have conveyed her exhaustion and stress because her argumentative father actually snapped his mouth shut.

"Fine."

"Thank you."

Taking his arm, she propelled him out the door and immediately breathed in the fresh, invigorating smell of spring. If only his yard didn't look so barren and awful.

"Why did you pull everything out, Dad?" she asked as they headed toward the sidewalk.

"Pull what out?"

"The roses, lilacs, azaleas, hibiscus . . ." She shook her head sadly. "The tulips would have been in bloom right now if you'd let them be. But now they're all gone, just like Mom."

"Exactly," came his curt answer, as if that explained everything.

"What's that supposed to mean?"

"It means she's not here anymore and neither are you. It's better with them gone."

His words had a tug-of-war effect on Cambri's heart, both paining it and touching it at the same time. She'd always known he missed her mother, but hearing him admit that he missed Cambri too was . . . surprising. And endearing. It made her almost forgive him for tearing out her mother's plants.

"You kept her pictures, her furniture."

He shrugged. "I realized I'd have to burn down the house to get rid of everything, and that seemed a little extreme, even for me. Sometimes I wish I could get the yard back, but then I come to my senses and remember I'm no gardener and couldn't keep it up anyway." He stopped to catch his breath, and Cambri could tell by the way he was leaning on her that he'd had enough.

"Let's turn back," she suggested.

He didn't argue, which meant that he really was tired. She held tight to his arm, feeling a camaraderie she'd never felt with her dad. She liked him this way.

"What do you say we invite Grandpa Cal and Jace over for dinner?" she suggested. Not only would it be nice to see them both, but if Cambri could corner Jace tonight, she could be back to being productive tomorrow.

"Only if you promise to grill some steaks," her father responded shortly. "I'm not about to feed anyone else what you've been feeding me lately."

Cambri leaned her head against his shoulder. "What about tilapia instead?"

"But I'm craving red meat."

"I'll put some food coloring in yours."

For the first time since Cambri's arrival, Harvey Blaine laughed. It was a good sound.

The chime of the doorbell caused Cambri's heartbeat to quicken. She drew in a deep breath and double-checked her appearance in the small, hallway mirror. She'd taken extra care with her hair and makeup and had pulled out a flattering mint green shirt that she'd been saving for a special occasion. Tonight, she wanted to make a good impression.

After another calming breath, Cambri opened the door with a ready smile. "Hey, Grandpa Cal." Her smile faltered slightly when she realized he was alone.

He offered one of his sympathetic looks. "Jace couldn't make it. Sorry, sweetie."

"Oh, no worries." She forced her smile back and gave him a quick hug. "I'm glad you're here."

"If your cooking's anything like your mother's, how could I say no?"

Cambri closed the door behind him, trying to push her disappointment aside. "I hate to break it to you, but no one can cook like my mother—least of all me. Tonight, you're going to get a very subpar meal."

"I doubt that. It smells delicious." A twinkle appeared in his eyes as he rubbed his hands together in anticipation. "Can't wait to try it."

Cambri linked her arm through his and led him back to the kitchen. Throughout dinner, she tried to put on a happy front and participate in the conversation, but her mind kept wandering in the direction of Jace. Why hadn't he come, or at least called to tell her himself? Did he hate her that much?

Cambri pushed the green beans around her plate with a frown. If he continued to avoid her, if he never let her explain—well, there wasn't much she could do about it. She'd just have to learn to live with it, the way she lived with a slightly crooked finger after she broke it during cheerleading practice.

Cal's hand patted hers, bringing her back to the present. "Your dad just challenged you to a game of chess," he said.

Cambri's frown deepened. Chess? She hated that game. Every time her father had coerced her into playing when she was younger, he questioned every move she made, making her feel like they were all wrong. Then out of the blue, he'd say "check mate" when she had no idea he was in a position to do that.

No. Things were just getting peaceful between them. She wasn't about to ruin it with a game of chess.

"I'll pass, thanks." She stood and started clearing the dishes. "I think I might go for a walk, if that's okay. I could use some air. Why don't you two play?"

Call patted his protruding belly. "I'd better get going too. That meal was delicious, Cambri. If I didn't know any better, I would have thought your mother had made it."

Cambri smiled her thanks, even though the meal had been a minor league effort. But sweet Cal was the last person in the world to ever admit that.

"You've always been such a toady," huffed her father to Cal. "That tasted nothing like one of Rose's meals. The fish was dry and the beans could have been put in a jar and sold as baby food."

"It's called tact, not toadying," Cal shot back. "And I happen to like my beans that way."

"Hogwash."

Cal threw down his napkin. "I wasn't planning to stay, but now I've changed my mind. Someone needs to bring you down a notch, and I suddenly want that person to be me. Where's the chess set?"

"Where it always is. In the hutch," Harvey shot back.

Cambri shook her head at the interchange as she finished rinsing the dishes. Then she grabbed her hoodie, said goodnight, and walked out into a brisk, April night. When she reached the sidewalk, she paused and looked around. Across the street, a few tulips swayed in the breeze as though they, too, wanted to get out and walk. Too bad for them they were stuck.

An invigorating sense of freedom lifted Cambri's mood as she strolled up the street. Budding branches looked ready to open any day now, with the shrubs and irises not far behind. Springtime in Bridger was her favorite time of year with all the flowering trees and blossoms that rained down every time the wind kicked up. She used to love to walk the street during those windstorms and feel the pattering of petals on her skin. It made her feel like she was in her own little fairyland where anything was possible.

A strange sort of wistfulness washed over her as she passed home after home of the people she'd once thought of as family. In only a few weeks, Cambri would be leaving, and while she was excited to get back to her job and her friends in Charlotte, part of her wished she could stay. She missed this place, the people, the slow way of life—a lot more than she'd realized.

As the sky darkened and the streetlights flickered on, Cambri pushed her hands into the pockets of her hoodie. She continued to walk, not caring about the chill, and eventually found herself hanging a left on Rose Street and strolling toward the one house she'd always thought of as hers. She paused and studied the home. The front room glowed lightly through the blinds, but the rest of the house matched the darkened sky. Cambri couldn't help but wonder who lived there. Who was updating it, and what plans did they have for the rest of the house, including the yard?

The flower beds had been stripped of all plant life, probably so the renovator could replace the siding, and the rest of the yard was becoming a jungle. Cambri couldn't help but picture a flagstone walkway with a Japanese maple, an Alpine evergreen, and some spirea and lilies. Over there she'd plant an autumn yellow bracken fern and a pink bleeding heart, along with a new maple tree. It would be a tamed sort of wildness. Beautiful.

The light in the front room flickered off, and the door opened. A woman about Cambri's age, with long strawberry blonde, hair jogged down the steps and stopped when she saw Cambri.

"Lydia?" Cambri asked. "Is that you?"

Lydia moved slowly forward, her eyebrows drawn together in confusion. "I'm sorry. Do I know you?"

"It's me, Cambri Blaine."

A wide smile appeared. "Cambri?" She strode forward and threw her arms around Cambri, reminding her of one of Grandpa Cal's hugs. He'd taught his granddaughter well. "It's been forever! How are you?"

"I'm good. How are you?" Cambri said, pulling back. "I had no idea you were still around."

A light breeze blew some strands of hair in Lydia's face, and she tucked it behind her ear then hugged her arms to her chest. "I never really left. I went to school in Ft. Collins and took a teaching job there. "

Cambri gestured to the home behind Lydia. "Well, it looks like you've done okay for yourself. That's got to be the most beautiful home in all of Bridger. I'm a little jealous."

Lydia glanced over her shoulder. "Oh no, that isn't my house. It's Jace's."

Cambri froze. What? Jace owned this house? The house she used to make him drive past on their way home from school so she could daydream about living in it one day? *He* was the one renovating it?

Her gaze traveled to the spot where the old maple used to stand. She pictured the tree as it had been six years earlier, with its large canopy shading the side of the road where Jace had stopped his old Mustang that day.

"Why do you like this house so much?" he'd asked. "It's so . . . old."

"It's got character," she'd said.

"You have a funny definition of character." He leaned over her to point out the window. "That shutter's missing, that one's all skiwampus, the siding looks like it's from the Dark Ages, and just look at the screen door. It's falling apart."

Cambri poked him in the ribs. "All it needs is a little TLC."

Jace shook his head in a *whatever* kind of way. His face had been so close and his eyes dark and beautiful. "You and your projects."

"What projects?"

"This house." He dropped his voice. "Me."

She laughed and pushed him away. "Please. You're hardly a project."

"I'm awkward, too skinny, and drive a baby blue mustang that is more rust than blue. I'm the guy in those movies who the beautiful, popular girl is challenged to fix." He grinned. "So far, you're failing."

He said it in a joking way, but there was a hint of honesty in his words, as though he actually believed it. Cambri wasn't okay with that. Impulsively, she kissed his cheek. "I'd never want to change you. I think you're perfect the way you are."

His gaze captured hers, and Cambri couldn't look away. He moved closer, and she didn't stop him. When she felt the warmth of his breath on her face and caught a whiff of mint, her heart pounded so hard she could feel the reverberations in her ears. She closed her eyes, his lips touched hers, and she—

"Earth to Cambri," Lydia cooed, waving a hand in front of Cambri's face.

Heat rushed to her face when she realized where her thoughts had headed—and right in front of Jace's sister. "I'm sorry. You caught me off guard. I didn't realize this was Jace's place."

Lydia looked confused. "You're not here to see him?"

"I was just out taking a walk and somehow ended up here."

A perfectly shaped eyebrow rose, as though Lydia didn't quite believe her. "Your dad's house is over a mile from here."

"I know, but your grandpa came over tonight, and he and my dad started a game of chess. I didn't really want to hang around, and a short walk wasn't going to cut it."

Lydia laughed. "You sound like me on their fly tying nights. I always find an excuse to leave."

"Oh," said Cambri. "Are you living with Grandpa Cal?" How like her friend to stay with him so he didn't get lonely. Yet another example of loyalty in the Sutton family.

Lydia's gaze dropped to the ground, and she shuffled her feet as if embarrassed. "After Mom and Dad moved away, it made the most sense. Grandpa had someone to look after him and keep his fridge stocked, and I got free rent. I'm saving up for a place of my own one day, but for now, life is really . . . good." The way she said it made it sound like she was trying to convince herself.

Cambri placed her hand on her friend's arm. "He's lucky to have you."

"Thanks." Lydia nodded toward the house. "I just dropped by to bring Jace some dinner. He met with a bunch of suppliers in Denver today and won't be home until late. Knowing him, he hasn't eaten much and will be starving by the time he gets back."

Oh, so that's why Jace couldn't make it to dinner. "That was nice of you." Not that Cambri was surprised at all. That was the Sutton way—always thinking about each other and everyone else they happened to know. Once upon a time, Cambri had been the recipient of a lot of kindnesses like that, and her heart now ached with a sense of loss.

Lydia shivered then cocked her head toward her car. "Want a ride back? It's kind of cold out here."

"I think I'll pass. I, uh . . . have some more thinking to do." Cambri suddenly felt vulnerable and uncertain and needed to sort out her thoughts and find a way to regroup. As much as she'd love to catch up with Lydia, now wasn't the time.

Lydia nodded in understanding. "I'll stop keeping you then. Just promise you won't leave town until we have a chance to hang out. I want to hear all about what's been going on with you." She gave Cambri another quick hug. "It's so great to see you."

"You too," said Cambri. "I'll call you."

"Okay." The door shut, the engine rumbled, and Lydia waved goodbye as she pulled from the driveway. Cambri watched until her tail lights disappeared then she shoved her hands into her pockets and gave the house one last look. It was time to start back. Time to refocus her thoughts on the life she'd made for herself in North Carolina. But instead of turning away, her feet carried her toward the house. She walked up the crumbling path and finally stopped on the cold, hard earth just outside the large front window. Although it was dark inside, if she pressed her nose against the glass, she could make out a staircase with white painted wooden slats and a dark stained handrail. What appeared to be a new hardwood floor spread through the front room and back into the dining area, and everything from paint cans to left over wooden planks cluttered a table beyond. It was still a work in progress, but the inside was shaping up to be as beautiful as the outside.

An engine rumbled in the distance, glittering stars reflected in the window, and Cambri waged a war in her heart. She'd gone to a great school, gained a valuable education, and now she had a wonderful, fulfilling job. Why did she feel like her life had veered off course? That she belonged here and not in North Carolina? It didn't make sense. Other than her father, there was nothing here for her in Bridger anymore. No job. No future. No life. Moving back would be nothing more than a constant, in-her-face reminder of what she'd given up.

This was her past. Charlotte was her future.

Seven

A peaceful feeling of home struck Jace as he drove into Bridger. It had been a long day of haggling with suppliers over raised prices and stressing about what it would mean for his business. He'd cut back everywhere he could, but it wasn't enough, and if prices continued to rise and his revenues stayed flat, in only a matter of years he'd have to cut his losses and close up shop. The thought made him ill.

Jace needed to decompress and get his mind on other things. He'd go home, eat whatever he could find, take a long, hot shower, and find a home improvement show on TV. Tomorrow, he'd worry about the store.

As he pulled into his driveway, he caught a movement out of the corner of his eye and slammed on the brakes. A woman stood outside his front window with her nose pressed to the glass. He leaned forward and squinted. Was that Cambri?

Ever so slowly, she twisted around, moving her hand up to shade her eyes against the light. Next to the darkness of her hair, her face looked pale, almost Snow White-ish. It was pulled back into a loose knot, with a few locks framing her face and deep, red lips. If there was a magic mirror around, it would probably decree Cambri as the fairest one of all.

Too bad Jace was no prince charming.

He quickly killed his engine and his lights with it, leaving Cambri standing in the darkness. She must have recognized his truck because she closed her eyes and shook her head, as though wishing the ground would swallow her whole.

A smile tugged at the corner of Jace's mouth. In all of his memories, Cambri had always faced life head-on without the typical insecurity or awkwardness that most teenagers experienced. But ever since she returned, or at least whenever Jace bumped into her, that confidence seemed to take a back seat to fluster. It was refreshing and even endearing, as much as he hated to admit it.

Jace slid from his truck and closed the door with a slam. He took a few steps toward her and stopped. "Stalking again, are we?"

She lifted her hands, palms facing up. "You caught me." She drew her lower lip into her mouth in a nervous gesture, as though she had no idea how to explain her current peeping Tom status. Finally, she shrugged. "It's not like I set out to spy on you. I was out wandering around and couldn't resist dropping by my favorite old house—which is now yours, I hear."

She made it sound like recent news, as though she'd just found out. "From whom?"

"Lydia. She was just leaving when I showed up." Cambri gnawed on her lower lip again before rushing on to say, "I'm sorry. I shouldn't have peeked, but you've done such a great job with the outside, I just wanted to see what the inside looked like."

"Oh." Jace wasn't sure how he felt about her liking the house. While the prideful part of him couldn't help but preen, another side wanted her to hate it—the way Eden would have hated him for updating her childhood home. This was his place now, and all the renovations he'd made had been to make it his home—not Cambri's. But now that she'd approved of the changes, she was back in everything, and Jace suddenly felt like he needed to make over his makeover just so it could be all his again.

Cambri shuffled her feet then waved her hand in a flippant gesture. "So there you have it—the story of how I inadvertently became a real stalker. Want to call the police now? I'll go without a fight if it means I don't have to stand here feeling stupid anymore."

There it was again—that charming insecurity that sneaked under the fence of his indifference and touched a tender spot in his heart. "Did you walk here?"

Another shuffle. Another shrug. "I didn't mean to walk this far. My feet just kept on going." She cringed. "I think I need to stop talking now. That sounded lame."

A snicker escaped Jace's mouth, and his gaze dropped to the ground. His foot scuffed against the crumbling walkway, dislodging a piece of concrete. He reached down to grab it then held it up for Cambri's inspection. "I always told you this place was a wreck."

"And yet you bought it." It was both a statement and a question.

Jace tossed the piece of concrete to the ground and shoved his hands into his pockets, looking up at the house. "It came on the market a few months back when I happened to be looking and it was pretty much my only option." He chuckled. "The one house I used to tease you about liking. And now I own it. Go figure."

"It's called karma." Cambri smiled. "Admit it. I was right. This place has character."

"Maybe." He smiled slightly, glancing her way. "It definitely reminds me of you."

She caught his gaze and held it, making Jace's heart pound in an uneven rhythm. "In a good way or bad?"

Whether it was the darkness of the night or the reminder of a time when he used to talk to Cambri about everything, Jace felt himself wanting to open up to her. But like a rusted hinge being pried open, the words didn't come as easy as they used to. "A little of both maybe. Mostly good, though. And yes, you were right, it does have great character."

Cambri stepped to his side and indicated the house. "You've made it beautiful—more so than I ever envisioned. I always knew you were talented from all the cool things you used to make in your shop classes—but this . . . this is impressive. It's very you."

Three little words, and suddenly the house was all his again. "Thanks."

"Did you have to kill the tree though?" Cambri smiled as she said it, but there was an underlying sadness in her voice that pricked Jace's heart.

But what else could he do? There was no disguising the tree, or changing it to make it Jace's and not hers. Every time he'd driven down Rose Street, that maple taunted him with the reminder of a perfect kiss gone way wrong and a friendship destroyed. It had to go. "The roots were making the sidewalk buckle."

She looked at the spot where it had once stood and shook her head sadly. "It was so big. So beautiful. So perfect."

And so in his face. "Your attachment to that tree wasn't healthy. You'll thank me for getting rid of it someday."

She cocked her head at him and lifted an eyebrow. "Just like you're now thanking me for accidentally driving your bullet bike into the pond?"

Jace frowned. "I'll never thank you for that. That was a travesty."

"And you accuse me of having an unhealthy obsession," she muttered.

"What are you talking about? You loved that bike too."

"Not enough to fish it out of the pond and hold a burial service for it."

"That bike was family." Jace shook his head, then chuckled at the memory. "It took all day to dig a hole big enough for that bike."

"I know. I helped! Remember?"

Jace did remember. Cambri, covered in dirt and sweat, glaring at him from the bottom of the hole. "This is taking forever," she'd said. "Why don't we just throw it in front of a semi just to break it down a little? Or better yet—have it cremated?"

"Is that what you'd want done to you after you die?" he'd countered.

"No." She wiped her matted hair away from her face. "I would have wanted you to leave me at the bottom of the pond," she grumbled. "Which is exactly where that bike should still be."

And that was why Jace had insisted on burying the bike. He got to spend the entire day with Cambri because of it. Even though it made him look overly attached to a hunk of metal, it had been worth it.

"I've always wondered if the new owners of our old house ever dug that up," said Jace. "It's not like we buried it that deep. All it would take was a good tiller to expose some of those rusted old remains."

Cambri shivered. "Don't say that. I can't stand the sound of grinding metal or metal scraping anything. It's almost as bad as fingernails on a chalkboard."

"You mean like a shovel grating against rock or the sound of car breaks grinding or—"

"Stop." Cambri clamped her hand over his mouth. "I almost forgot how evil you can be."

"Almost?" Jace said, his voice muffled by her hand. He'd meant it as a joke, but the humor drained from her face as she met and returned his gaze. Her hand slowly dropped from his mouth, and she looked away.

Jace would give anything to know what she was thinking.

She cleared her throat, and her voice took on a forced brightness. "Hey, you don't, by chance, take on side projects, do you? I was thinking of having my dad's old shed rebuilt. It's falling apart, and he could really use a bigger one." Her eyes met his again, looking anxious. "I'd pay you, of course."

Her question was met with silence, mostly because Jace didn't know how to answer. Once again, his shoe scuffed against the sidewalk, and he watched the concrete crumble. Like the digging of that ridiculous hole for his bike, he wanted to say yes, to spend more time with her. He wanted to remember the old and discover the new, but she was leaving, and Jace had learned long ago that the only thing she wanted from him was friendship. He didn't think he could go back to that.

"I'm actually pretty busy right now with this house. But I know a guy who'd be interested if you want his name and number."

"Oh, um, yeah . . ." Did she sound disappointed? "That'd be great."

Jace nodded toward the house. "C'mon in, and I'll get it for you. I'll even let you take a look around—in a non-creepy, legal way."

"Ha ha," she said.

Inside, Jace watched Cambri as she walked slowly around the bare room. She ran her hand up and down the smooth banister, across the white fireplace mantle, and briefly touched the gray semi-gloss paint before turning back to him.

"It's beautiful," she said. "Did you do all this work yourself?"

He nodded. "I like to stay busy. It keeps me out of trouble."

"Since you were always such a troublemaker," she joked.

"I was," said Jace. "Mr. Badboy himself."

Cambri laughed at that, and Jace stiffened. He hadn't heard that laugh since she'd returned. It was her real laugh—the one that used to warm him up from the inside out and make his days happier. The one that brightened the bare, dimly lit room now. The one that would be walking out the door in just a few minutes.

She wandered into the kitchen and ran her fingers across the ugly orange laminate countertop. Other than the floor, Jace hadn't done anything to the kitchen yet.

"What do you plan to do in here?" she asked.

"Leave it as is," came his answer. "I'm a sucker for that orange."

Cambri laughed again, and the room brightened a little more. Even the countertops looked a little less hideous. "You could always paint the cabinets black and make it Halloween-ish since you love that holiday so much," she teased again. Jace had once made the mistake of telling her that he hated Halloween and all the gruesome costumes that came with it. From that point forward, she'd shown up on his doorstep every October 31, wearing the most hideous costume she could come up with.

Jace leaned against the counter and folded his arms. "I should enlarge some of those pictures of you in that Joker costume to hang on the wall." Thinking about it still gave him the heebie geebies. The blackened eyes, the white, crackled face, the bright red lips that bled beyond the point where lips should bleed. And her hair—all scraggly and oily looking.

"I used to dress up as a princess or maid or movie star," said Cambri with a wistful smile. "But then I got to know you and . . . things changed."

"I'll say. I brought out the worst in you."

Cambri looked down and picked at the corner of the counter, where a bit of laminate had come loose. "Maybe when it came to Halloween costumes. But otherwise I really liked myself when I was with you. With everyone else, I always felt like I had to say the right thing, look the right way, and fit the right image. But with you, I could be goofy, stupid, ugly, and silly, and I knew you wouldn't care. You liked me no matter what."

She peeked at him in a hesitant way, and a palpable energy filled the space between them. *Why did you leave then? Why didn't you return my calls? Why didn't you keep in touch? And why did you kiss me back?* Because she had. It had been tentative at first, but then her fingers were in his hair and her lips moving hard and hungry against his. For a brief moment, Jace had felt like he'd somehow managed to get the one girl he never really believed he could ever get.

But then Cambri froze, slowly backed away, and asked him to drive her home. Two days later, she'd left town and that was that. No explanation, no goodbye, nothing. Just gone.

The feelings of way back when slammed into Jace once again, feeling fresh and raw. Six years, and he still hadn't put it behind him. Six years, and she could still make him feel this way. His jaw clenched in frustration.

"Listen, Jace." Cambri was back to picking at the laminate with her fingernail. "I know this is long overdue, but I owe you an apology."

Jace swallowed. "No need. It's all water under the bridge now."

Her head shook. "Maybe for you it is, but not for me. It never has been. I know I have no right to ask you anything, but I'd really appreciate it if you'd hear me out." She paused. "Please."

With a sigh, Jace dropped down on a barstool and nodded.

The mole to the side of her lips twitched a moment, and then she began. "When Mom died, everything changed, including Dad. He went from being the person who stayed out of my way and let Mom deal with me to someone who was always in my way. Nothing I did seemed to satisfy him. He hated that I was a cheerleader. He didn't like my friends—except you, of course. And when I started talking about going across the country to school, he got after me about that too. He couldn't understand why I wanted to go to Penn State over CSU. It didn't matter that Penn State had the program I wanted to attend and CSU didn't. And the more he pushed, the more stifled I felt."

She shook her head, as if to clear her thoughts. "Then there was you. My best friend. The one person in my life who never pushed and always wanted what was best for me. You even helped me research colleges and landscape architect programs, remember?"

He remembered. Remembered inwardly cringing when Penn State gradually rose to the top of her wish list. But Jace had never said anything to discourage her. If that's where she wanted to go, he'd help her get there.

"But then you kissed me." She looked so troubled, even confused. "It caught me off guard and made me realize how much I cared about you and how easy it would be to say no to college and do exactly what my father wanted me to do. And that scared me. I didn't want his dreams to become my dreams, and all of a sudden, it felt as though both of you were ganging up on me, trying to get me to stay in a place that I just . . . couldn't."

Jace leaned forward, resting his elbows on the counter. "I wasn't trying to make you stay. I was trying to let you know how I felt. I never expected—or wanted—you to give up your dreams for me."

Cambri nodded, her voice quiet. "I know. I was just so mixed up that I needed to get away and take some time to think. But when I moved to Pennsylvania, I was a country girl in a big city, lonely and intimidated. I was afraid that if I called, if I heard your voice, I'd jump on the next flight home. So I didn't. And the more time that passed, the harder it became to pick up the phone. Then one day, I decided it had been too long and wouldn't matter anymore." She paused. "But I was wrong. I'm so sorry, Jace. I should have never left like that. I should have never let you slip from my life. It's something I'll always regret."

The floor creaked, sounding loud in the silence. Jace didn't know what to say—or think, for that matter. What did a six-year-old apology mean now? Was this Cambri's way of getting closure, or did she want to renew the friendship and keep in touch? What did she want from him? What did he want from her?

Kiss-and-make-ups were supposed to happen before six years later. Before someone makes a life somewhere else.

The silence continued, getting more uncomfortable with each passing second. Finally, Cambri placed her hand over his. "I always thought this house deserved an amazing owner. I'm glad it's you. Goodnight, Jace."

He watched as she zipped up her hoodie and walked out the front door, closing it softly behind her. The air was cold and the night dark. He couldn't let her walk home at this hour. Jace strode to the door and pulled it open.

"Cam." Her shortened name came natural to him, the way it had in high school. "Want a ride home?"

She looked over her shoulder and nodded. "I'd love one."

During the ride back to her father's, Jace was quiet and contemplative, and the air crackled with unsaid words. When he pulled to a stop in front of her father's house, he threw his truck into park. "Thanks for explaining," he finally said. "It's nice to finally understand why you did what you did."

"I should have told you a long time ago. I'm sorry I didn't."

Jace glanced her way and shrugged. "No worries. It's over."

"Yeah, yeah. Water under a bridge, I know."

He picked at something on his steering wheel, feeling restless and confused. "When are you heading back?"

"Not sure." Cambri glanced at the house. "Soon, or else I might be out of a job. But I can't help worrying about Dad. What if he doesn't keep eating healthy or getting the right amount of exercise? Things between us are better than they've ever been, and if I leave . . ." She let the words trail off.

Jace cocked his head and studied her, feeling like they were back to where they were six years ago, with her dad still pulling her to stay. Jace wasn't about to join in. "Don't let your dad keep you here. He's got friends who will look after him—including me. You have a life somewhere else, and you can't put it on hold forever."

"Like you didn't put your life on hold for your grandfather?" Cambri said, her voice so quiet he almost didn't hear.

Jace shifted to face her. "I didn't put my life on hold for him. I've always loved it here, and when my parents decided to move and pass the business down to me, it was an easy thing to accept because I wanted it. Trust me, I'm more selfish than loyal."

Cambri shook her head as though she didn't believe him. "I'm glad things worked out for you."

"And I'm glad things worked out for you."

When an awkward silence started creeping in again, she yanked on the door handle. "I guess I'll see you around?"

"I'd say that's a pretty safe bet," he joked. "You are stalking me."

"Right." Cambri smiled slightly. "Maybe I'll peek in your windows sometime soon then."

He watched her for a moment, feeling like this was a goodbye. A better goodbye then before, but his heart still wrenched at the thought of not seeing her again. "Or you can knock. If I'm there, I'll answer."

Her smile grew larger. "I'd like that. Night, Jace." She hopped from the car and sauntered toward her house. On the front porch, she turned and lifted a hand.

Jace took that as his cue and left.

"Nickelback!" The non-expletive was the first thing Cambri heard as she walked inside, shutting the door quietly behind her. Although her heart still felt heavy, it had a lightness to it that had been missing for a long time. She should have talked to Jace years ago.

"I'm telling you, I didn't cheat," countered Grandpa Cal. "How could I? You were sitting there the entire time."

"You distracted me with all those stories, that's how," said Harvey. "I never lose at chess."

"Only because I always let you win to avoid an argument like this."

"Then why didn't you let me win today?" her father countered.

"To teach you a lesson in humility, remember?" Grandpa Cal said. "I should have known better. You and humility go together about as well as pickles and lemonade."

"Spitwicks." Cambri walked into the kitchen and found her father jabbing a finger on the table to make a point. "I am the best chess player in the county, and you and I both know it."

"Looks like I just kicked you out of that spot."

Her father pushed his chair back at the same time Cambri decided it was time to intervene. "I'm glad to see you're both good sports when it comes to losing"—she shot her father a warning look—"and winning"—she turned her expression on Grandpa Cal. "Your late wives would be so proud of you both right now."

That seemed to shut them up. At least until her father pointed a finger at Cal. "You and me, next week. Same time and place."

"I'll be here."

Cambri rolled her eyes, making a mental note to hide the chess game before then. She clapped her hands together and forced a smile to her face. "Now that that's settled, it's time for your meds, Dad."

Her father frowned, and Cal grabbed his jacket. He gave Cambri a side hug and pecked her on the forehead. "Thanks for dinner, Cambri. It hit the spot."

"Yeah, like an arrow in the gut," her father grumbled.

"Never you mind him," said Cal. "They don't make medicine strong enough to cure his surliness."

"I never do," said Cambri with a smile.

She walked him to the door, waved goodbye, then returned to her father. After handing him his meds, she leaned her hip casually against the table. "I've been thinking about your yard. How would you feel about me giving it a bit of a makeover before I leave?"

"Before you leave?" He eyed her with a look she couldn't interpret. Wariness perhaps? Disappointment?

Cambri sighed and pulled out a chair, sitting across from him. "I have to go back, Dad. My life is there, not here."

"Your life is where you want it to be."

"Right now I want it to be there." Although the words sounded firm and believable, Cambri's heart still wavered. But that was only because she was here. Once she returned to Charlotte, she'd transition easily back into her old life and start looking forward instead of back.

Her father let out a breath and leaned back in his chair. "No good ever came from arguing with you. If that's really what you want, then that's what it will be."

Cambri eyed him with a mixture of respect and gratitude. Where was this attitude in high school? Or when she'd first come back? It was so much easier to feel close to him when he took a step back and supported her even though he disagreed.

"But I don't have to like it," he added brusquely.

Cambri placed her hand over his. "Believe it or not, I'm going to miss you. But I'm not leaving yet, and I'd love to give you a goodbye present this time. I'm good at what I do, so let me make your yard beautiful before I go."

"I doubt I'll be able to keep it up."

"The doctor says you need exercise," she countered. "Pushing a lawn mower around the yard and pulling a few weeds will be good for you."

He grunted and folded his arms. "I guess it won't hurt to spruce it up a little. If your mother were still alive, she'd like that."

Cambri heard the slight catch in his voice when he talked about her mother. In his own way, he'd loved her deeply, just like Cambri had. She felt her heart lighten a little bit more. "Yes. Yes, she would."

That night, as Cambri booted up her laptop to work on the design for her boss, her mind opened, and a week of pent-up creativity came gushing out.

She quickly sketched her ideas out on paper then got to work.

Eight

Cambri blinked at her bedroom ceiling as the first rays of morning sunlight filtered through the blinds. Even though she'd spent half of the night working on the landscape design plan, she'd never felt so invigorated. She'd look it over one last time this morning, then send it off to her boss two days before the deadline. And then she'd get to work on her father's yard. A slow smile stretched across her face at the prospect of a new day with a new project on her plate. She couldn't wait to get started.

In no time at all, she'd clicked Send, dressed in the oldest jeans she'd brought, made her father some oatmeal, and headed outside. An early spring chill made her shiver, but she didn't care. Cambri had work to do, and she'd begin with her father's poor excuse for a shed. It took the majority of the morning to clean it out and try to organize everything.

Her father came out close to noon, asking what she was up to.

"Just reorganizing, Dad. Don't worry about it."

His expression wary, he eyed the boxes of fishing gear

that she'd collected from the shed. "I expect everything to be put back the way you found it when you're done. Otherwise I won't be able to find anything."

Cambri lifted an eyebrow. He could actually find stuff in the chaos that was his shed before? Good thing she snapped a few pictures, because unbeknownst to her father, this shed was coming down.

"You're just going to have to trust me," she said, shooing him back inside.

After lunch, Cambri coerced him into going on a mandatory walk before parking him in front of the TV with his favorite Discovery show on, with the volume turned up loud. Then she returned to the backyard, hefted a sledgehammer, and started bringing down the house—or shed, in this instance. The fact that a few swings of the hammer could do so much damage was proof that it needed to come down.

"What in Sputnik's name are you doing?" boomed her father from the back patio. Evidently Cambri hadn't turned up the volume enough.

She set the sledgehammer down and wiped at the perspiration on her forehead. "What does it look like I'm doing? I'm putting your shed to rest."

He charged toward her. "Where do you propose I keep all my fishing gear now?"

"In the garage, for now. Then in the new shed I'm planning to put up over there." Cambri pointed to the side of the house, adjacent to the garage. She'd already found the perfect pre-fabricated shed online and planned to order it through Sutton's Hardware later that afternoon, along with the supplies she'd need for the water feature.

"What about all that gravel?" he said, referring to the iffy foundation he'd used for his old shed.

"I'm getting rid of it. The concrete pad on the side of the

house is a way better location for a shed. It will be easier access for you too."

He didn't look pacified. "What about this space? What's it going to become? A garden to grow all those fresh fruits and veggies you've been trying to shove down my throat lately?"

"No, it's going to be a water feature. Your garden will go over there, where it's sunnier."

"A water what?"

"Feature," Cambri said. "It will be like having a little stream of your very own."

Her father's eyes widened and his frown deepened. "I don't want some frou-frou waterfall back here. I'm not an old woman!"

"I said stream, not waterfall, and I know you're not an old woman. You're a cantankerous old man. Now stop being so resistant to change and go finish your show. I've got this."

Glowering, her father stalked toward the house, muttering about how that's what he got for giving a woman the go-ahead to make a few improvements. "She's just like her mother," he grumbled.

"Thanks," Cambri said under her breath, feeling a connection to her mom that she hadn't experience in awhile. With a satisfied smile, she finished tearing down what was left of the shed. Several wheelbarrow loads later, the majority of the gravel was transported to the back of her father's truck, revealing a completely clean ten-by-ten space for Cambri to work with. She smiled at the prospect of what it would become.

"Wow, someone's been busy."

At the sound of Jace's voice, Cambri spun around, feeling suddenly self-conscious. Her hand flew up to tuck a few stray locks of hair behind her ear. She could only imagine how filthy and horrible she looked, though she wondered why she cared. She never used to before. "What are you doing here?"

His cocked his head toward the house. "Your dad called. Said I needed to get over here right away and put a stop to all your girly plans. He wants a few shrubs added to the front yard and that's it."

Cambri suddenly felt like dropping the sledgehammer on her father's big toe. All day long, she'd been working hard to create something more functional and beautiful for her father. But could he find at least one thing to appreciate about her plans or discuss it with her in a mature, adult way? Even ask to see her quickly drawn out plans or offer any sort of compromise? No. Instead, he calls on *loyal* Jace to talk some sense into his daughter.

Maybe it was her exhaustion, but Cambri's blood started to simmer. "A few shrubs?" she said, her voice escalating with every word. "He wants a few shrubs, and that's it?"

Jace eyed her with a wary expression. "I'm just the messenger."

"Great. Then you can give my dad this message: Tell him it's either a water feature and a new shed, or a yard full of the frilliest, most colorful perennials I can find!"

Jace's lips lifted into a smile. "That's very mature of you."

Cambri chose to ignore the fact that she'd just accused her father of the same thing. "He started it!" she said, jabbing a finger toward the house. When she saw her father peeking through the slats in the kitchen window, she threw down her work gloves and stormed toward the house. The slats immediately fell closed, and the click of the back door lock sounded.

She froze. Unbelievable. He'd actually locked her out.

Cambri continued forward, ready to pound on the back door until her father let her in, but a strong arm caught her around the waist, easily stopping her progress. "Let me go!" she said, squirming to free herself from Jace's grip.

"Calm down, Cam," he breathed into her ear, sending shivers down her spine. "What are you going to do, break down the door?"

Hmm . . . not such a bad idea. Cambri twisted her head around. "Where did that sledgehammer go?"

Jace chuckled, pulling her against him. "What did that door ever do to you?" More warm breath, more shivers. Man, he felt good.

"It locked." Cambri's voice came out sounding weak and breathless.

His chuckle became a laugh, reminding Cambri how wonderful it sounded. When she stopped squirming, he loosened his grip and stepped in front of her, his hands still on her waist. "Why don't you tell me what you have in mind for back here? If you can convince me it's a good plan, it'll be two against one."

Cambri didn't answer right away. She liked his hands where they were, and once she agreed, he'd move them. But she couldn't exactly keep quiet forever either.

"Deal," she finally said.

Just like she expected, he dropped his hands. "Okay. I'm all yours."

She blinked up at him, feeling her heart drop to her toes. "All mine?" She didn't mean to actually say the words—especially not in that lovesick, breathless way—but they were out before she could stop them.

"Yours?" His brows furrowed together.

"You said, 'I'm all yours.'"

The corner of his mouth tugged up. "No, I said 'I'm all ears.'"

Nice, Cam, real nice. Now she was both a stalker *and* a wannabe Valentine. "Oh. Right. Ears." Too bad hers weren't working properly.

A knowing smile on his face, Jace cocked his head

toward the spot where the shed used to stand. "What's going there?"

Glad for an excuse not to wallow in embarrassment, Cambri sighed. "Dad loves fishing, so I thought I'd put in a small stream, some flagstone pavers, a tree, and some shrubs scattered around. It would be the perfect spot for a hammock. The shed, on the other hand, will work better against the house over there."

Jace nodded slowly, as though considering it. "A water feature would be cool, and a hammock even better. And you're right, it does make more sense to keep the shed out of sight and on the existing concrete pad."

"Thank you." Cambri felt like hugging him. "Why can't my dad see that?"

"Because he's stubborn and likes to be contrary."

Cambri threw up her hands. "Well, now what? As much as I'd love to show him that I can be equally stubborn, I don't want to do anything that's really going to upset him, and this is his yard. So, do I hire someone to pour a slab back here, replace the shed, and forget the water feature?" She frowned, not liking that option at all. If her father would just let her do it, she was positive he'd love the end result.

Jace glanced at the house, looking amused. "What do you say we let your father cool off and go order that shed? We have a few catalogs at the store."

Wait, he was offering to come with her? Cambri blinked at him, tempted to take him up on it. But then she remembered his house. "Thanks, but I'm sure you have better things to do with your time. I'll stop by the store a little later, after I've calmed down and can make my dad see reason."

"My projects can wait." It sounded so final, as though no amount of arguing would change his mind. Jace would help her whether she liked it or not.

Cambri's stomach flip-flopped.

"Now that I think about it," Jace said, rubbing his chin. "Last fall, Larry brought back a waterfall pump he'd ordered through a catalog and didn't end up using. It's a decent size, and I bet it would work great for this project."

"You still have it? Why didn't you send it back?"

He shrugged. "It was past the return date."

"And yet you let Larry return it." It was a statement, not a question, because of course Jace did. He was the sort of guy who'd take a loss so someone else wouldn't have to. A lump formed in her throat.

"It wasn't a big deal. I figured I could resell it in the spring," he said. "But if you think it will work for this and can take it off my hands, it's yours. I'll even help you build it."

"I thought you had a lot going on with your house?"

His eyes met hers in a look that made her heart skip. "It'll wait."

Of all the guys Cambri had dated over the years, none were half so good as Jace Sutton. How could she have walked away from him before? How could she walk away from him now?

He's not yours to walk toward or away from, came the sad reminder. It was true. That ship had already sailed, and no amount of hoping or watching the horizon would bring it back. She'd messed up, and that was that.

Cambri cleared her throat, steering her mind toward slightly less depressing thoughts. "As much as I'd love to put a stream back here, I really don't think Dad would have gone to the effort to get you over here if he wasn't that opposed to it. Maybe I'll just plant a tree, bury two posts for a hammock, and call it good. A water feature would be a pain to build anyway."

Jace must have caught the wistfulness in her voice because his arm came around her shoulders, and he directed her toward his truck. "The Cambri I know wouldn't give up so easily. Where's the girl who was about to break down her dad's door with a sledgehammer or plant a bunch of perennials?" he teased.

"She's sick of fighting with him, so she's giving up." She stopped and looked up at him, feeling deflated all of a sudden. "No matter what I do or how hard I try, I'll never be good enough for him, will I? I'll never be you."

Jace spun her around to face him. "What are you talking about?"

"You know exactly what I'm talking about. You're the loyal one with your head screwed on straight, and I'm the disloyal screw-up."

"You? A screw-up?" Jace's lips twitched for a moment then straightened, as he realized she wasn't joking around. "I don't get how you could think that. You're beautiful, determined, motivated, successful, *and* loyal. You wouldn't be here if you weren't. And if that's your definition of a screw-up, then yeah, I guess you are one."

"Gee thanks," Cambri said.

He drew her into a hug, holding her close and reminding her how wonderful it felt to be hugged by him. "Your dad loves you, Cam. The only reason he acts that way or says what he does is because he's afraid of losing you again. It was hard for him when you left before, and it's going to be hard for him when you leave again. This is just his way of trying to protect himself from getting hurt. I mean, think about it. He already lost his wife. He doesn't want to lose his daughter too. He just has a more ornery way of showing that."

Cambri simultaneously laughed and sniffed. His words rang true, easing the pain and restoring the good. She kept her arms tight around him, refusing to let go. "How do you do that? No matter what happens or how badly I mess up, you've always been able to make me feel better. Even when Mom died . . ." She shook her head, remembering the pain.

"I honestly don't know how I would have made it through that without you. I've really missed you." *And don't want to live without you anymore.*

His response wasn't immediate, but it did come. "I've missed you too." Was it her, or did his arms tighten ever so slightly?

"What do you say we go check out the sheds and pump now?" He loosened his grip, bringing Cambri back to the harsh reality that he wasn't hers to hold.

She stepped away and glanced at the locked house once more, still not sure that was the right course of action. "Tell you what. If you convince my dad to let me do it, I'll let you help built it." If anyone could talk him into it, Jace could.

"You'll *let* me help?" Jace laughed. "Sheesh, I walked right into that one, didn't I?"

"Don't worry. It's an easy out. There's no way you'll ever get him to agree to it."

"That sounds like a challenge."

"It is."

"You know I never back down from a challenge."

"That's my hope."

He laughed again and headed toward the house with that confident stride of his. The click of the lock sounded, the door opened, and Jace disappeared inside. Cambri rolled her eyes. Of course her father would let *Jace* inside. The toad.

Ten minutes later, Jace emerged with a triumphant grin. "Ready to go?" he asked.

Cambri stared. "No way. How did you do that?"

His grin widened. "I told him we'd stock the stream with fish."

Nine

Despite Cambri's protests, Jace put all his home improvement projects on hold so he could help out every evening after work—and some afternoons when Sutton Hardware was a little slow. Every time Cambri mentioned her guilt at keeping him away from his own work, he'd always say, "You have a deadline, I don't." And no amount of coercion would change his mind, not that Cambri put up much of a fight. When the familiar sound of his truck pulled into the driveway, the day seemed to brighten. He made the work fun and the hours pass like seconds.

Gone was the awkward tension, and in its place bloomed something sturdier and deeper than their old high school friendship. Cambri had never felt so close to anyone, and her heart ached every time she thought of leaving.

On top of that, Cambri's relationship with her father was better than ever. Every so often, when she was replanting the front yard, he'd come out, walk around, then silently nod his approval. A few times, he took a seat on the steps and asked questions about what she was doing. He ate the food she made without grumbling and didn't argue when it was time for their daily walk around the block. He even remembered a few of her mother's plants that Cambri had forgotten.

By the following Saturday, the yard had been restored to a younger version of its former self. The electrical line had been run, the area for the stream had been excavated, and the liner and pump were in place. All that was left was to test it and arrange the boulders that had been delivered the day before.

As Cambri carried some shrubs from the back of her father's pick-up to the soon-to-be stream, the sun warmed her back at the same time a light breeze chilled her arms. The day would be a beautiful one, and Cambri couldn't wait to turn the plastic-lined trench into a beautiful stream.

The sound of a familiar engine rumbled in the driveway, followed by the slamming of a door. A welcoming smile touched her lips as she turned around.

"You didn't test it without me, did you?" Dressed in work jeans and a loose-fitting t-shirt, Jace lifted the last shrub from the truck and walked toward her with an easy smile.

"No." Cambri couldn't help but admire his strong arms or the way his damp hair glistened in the morning sunlight. "As promised, I waited for you, though I did fill the reservoir. And guess what? No leaks!"

"Good." He set the plant on the ground and rubbed his hands together in anticipation. "Let's do this then."

Cambri knelt down and fingered the switch they'd installed the day before. "Ready?"

"Fingers crossed it works."

Holding her breath, she flipped the switch, then grinned when a low murmuring sounded, signaling the pump had activated. Soon, water gurgled and rushed down the slight hill they'd created, looking more like a Slip 'N Slide than a stream.

"It works!" Cambri leapt up, clapped her hands together, then skipped over to Jace and threw her arms around him. "Thank you, thank you, thank you! This is so cool!"

Jace's arms tightened around her, lifting the heels of her sneakers off the ground as he hugged her back. "You're acting like a kid who just built her first Lego set. I thought you've designed a bunch of these before."

"Designed—yes. Built—no. I just tell a crew where to put it then admire it when it's all done. "

"Ah, so you're one of *those* bosses," he teased. Although he pulled back slightly, his hands were still on her waist, sending a happy shiver up her spine.

"I help with the planting," she said.

"How? By telling them where to dig the holes?"

She slugged him lightly on the arm. "No. By digging some of the holes myself." Okay, so it never turned out to be that many, but when they were under a tight deadline, she'd always step in to help out.

"Oh, so you're obviously a skilled digger."

"The best," she lied. Actually, she was horrible, especially when the ground was hard and rocky.

"Can't wait to see how good." He grinned, nodding toward the plants waiting near the stream. "From the sounds of it, you won't need my help today. Maybe I'll just hang out on one of those patio seats, sip a lemonade, and observe."

"Yeah right." Jace was incapable of being idle when there was something that needed doing. "Ten bucks says you can't sit still for more than five minutes."

He chuckled. "You're right. I probably couldn't. Besides, I cleared out my schedule today, so I'm all *yours*." He emphasized the last word, reminding her of her Freudian slip from the week before. Every chance he could, he found a way to bring it up in one way or another.

Cambri rolled her eyes then poked him in the chest with her finger. "You'd better be all ears too, because I have a lot of ordering to do."

He laughed then nodded toward his truck. "Your shed came in this morning."

"It did?" Cambri craned her neck to look around him. "Do you think we'll have time to set it up today?"

"No," he said. "That can wait until Monday. I took the day off, so don't worry. We'll get it done before you leave."

Did he have to remind her? Cambri hated thinking about leaving on Tuesday. It was too soon. "But—"

"No buts. Today, we're going to place those boulders, plant the rest of the shrubs, and pour the concrete for the hammock posts. Then we're going out for dinner tonight to celebrate a job well done." He shot her an uncertain look. "Assuming you're available, that is."

Cambri's heart skipped a beat, possibly even two, even though she wasn't sure how to interpret the invitation. Was he asking her out on a date-date, or was it really just a celebratory dinner and nothing to get excited about? Was he inviting her father as well?

"Unless you don't want to," Jace said. "I can always ask your dad instead."

So it was just her. The thought thrilled her.

"I'd love to go." The words came out rushed, sounding like Cambri was afraid he'd rescind the invitation. She drew in a quick breath and forced herself to slow down. "But only if it's on me. I owe you big-time for all your help."

"I'll say." His mouth lifted into a half smile. "But I'll collect another time. I issued the invite, so tonight's on me."

"But—"

"I told you, no buts. Besides, are you really going to argue with me after all I've done for you?"

Cambri's eyes narrowed. "That's exactly why I'm arguing with you! I should be the one to pay."

"If you'd wanted to pay, then you should have done the asking," he said. "Since I beat you to it, I get to decide where we go and who's paying."

"And where are we going?"

"I was thinking Fort Collins for sushi. We can tell your dad we already caught the fish from the stream and ate it for dinner so we don't have to follow through on our promise to stock it."

"Very funny," said Cambri. "And you're kidding about the sushi thing too, right? Because I have this phobia of eating raw fish."

"Yeah, I know," he joked. "That's what you get for not asking first."

"Okay, fine." She shrugged, acting as though she didn't care. "But if it were up to me, I'd take you to Burgers On High and get you a double-decker with sweet potato fries." That had been Jace's favorite place to eat in high school. Was it still?

He grinned. "But you've never liked that place."

It was true. The burgers were greasy, and Cambri had never been a sweet-potato-fry fan. But it was better than raw fish. "My taste buds have matured over the years," she said. "I now love sweet potato fries."

"Liar."

Cambri loved that he still knew her so well. "Do they still have a live band on Saturday nights?"

"Yeah."

"That's good enough for me. We can go there for old times' sake. What do you say?"

For a moment, his eyes deepened with something that went beyond humor. But then he dropped his gaze to his feet and scuffed at the grass. "Yeah, okay. Burgers On High it is."

"Great. Then I'm paying," said Cambri.

He shook his head. "Let's save that fight for when we get there. Otherwise, we'll be arguing all day long."

"Okay, just promise not to tell Dad where we're going. He'll insist I bring him back a burger, and he's not allowed to eat those anymore."

"It'll be our secret."

For the next couple of hours, they placed boulders and rocks, shifted them around to wherever Cambri thought they'd look good, then shifted them again when they didn't. Jace teased her about giving manual labor a whole new meaning, and she teased him about it being *free* manual labor.

When Jace finally placed the last boulder, Cambri took a step back and inspected their work with a critical eye. It looked awesome. Better than she'd hoped. "I love it," she pronounced.

Jace quirked an eyebrow. "You sure? Because you're way pickier than I remember—not to mention indecisive—so I'm having a hard time believing that we're actually done."

Cambri responded by splashing him with a handful of water.

Jace splashed her back, and a water fight ensued. When Jace grabbed the hose and sprayed her with frigid water, Cambri's laughter rang out. She tried to wrestle it away from him, and in the end they both ended up drenched. Although Cambri shivered from the chill, she couldn't remember the last time she'd had that much fun.

"You two planning on getting any work done today?" called Harvey's voice from the back porch. He looked more pleased than upset.

"Yes sir," Jace answered. "Just needed to soften the ground a bit to make planting easier."

Cambri snickered, then tried to cover it up by placing her fist over her mouth and clearing her throat. Jace shot her a way-to-give-us-away look, making her snicker some more.

Her father gestured toward the house. "I've already made me a tuna sandwich on wheat, and there's extra inside if you two get hungry. I'm heading out for my afternoon walk, so feel free to get some actual work done now." Then he disappeared, leaving Cambri staring after him with her mouth hanging open.

He'd made them lunch? He was going for a walk all on his own? "Who was that man, and what did he do with my dad?"

Jace pointed a finger at Cambri. "Let that be a lesson to you. If a crotchety old man can change, anyone can."

Cambri laughed and dropped the hose. "I'm freezing. Why don't we go make some tuna sandwiches and dry off for a bit?"

"Sounds good to me."

Cambri retrieved some towels while Jace made the sandwiches, and by the time her father returned from his walk, they were back in the yard, ready to plant shrubs and mix concrete. Jace dug the post holes, while Cambri arranged the shrubs. Once she had them situated to her satisfaction, she started planting.

"Out of curiosity, where did you get those shrubs? I don't recognize most of them."

Cambri squinted up at him. "I would have bought them from your store, but Sutton's Hardware doesn't have that great of a selection, so I've been getting most of them from a nursery in Fort Collins. I hope that's okay."

"No worries," he said. "I know we have a limited selection. We've been stocking our small nursery with the same plants every year, but I don't know what else to do. I'm not familiar enough with plants to know what will sell well and what won't."

"I'd be happy to give you some suggestions if you'd like," said Cambri.

"Yeah, I'd appreciate that."

She gestured toward the stream. "It's the least I could do after all you've done to help me."

He planted his shovel in the earth and rested his elbow on top of it. "About that. I was sort of hoping I could convince you to draw up some plans for my yard. Not before you go, or anything, just sometime when you can spare a few minutes. It doesn't have to be fancy, but I really like what you've done here and would love something similar in my yard."

"Are you kidding? I'd love to." Did he actually consider that a favor? Already, Cambri's mind spun with ideas and plans. A flagstone walkway, a new maple tree, evergreens mixed with a few perennials, and a dash of lush. "Your yard's so small, it won't take me long to come up with a design. Maybe I could even stay another week to help you get going on it." She'd actually love nothing more. Another week with Jace—

"Cambri." He leveled her a look. "You've already pushed your departure date back a week for your dad. There's no way I'm letting you push it back again. I'm sure you're needed home."

Home.

The word had been on Cambri's mind a lot lately. Was Charlotte really her home? It didn't feel like it at the moment and maybe never really had. But Jace was right. At some point, Cambri needed to go back. Her job and life were there, and she couldn't keep postponing her stay indefinitely just because she wanted to. Besides, Dillon had already been more than generous to give her as much time away as he had. She knew it hadn't been easy for him to keep her up-to-date on all the meetings she'd missed.

She nodded. "Okay. I'll get you a plan as soon as I get back."

"Hey, no rush, okay? Just whenever."

"Got it."

He grabbed the shovel, giving her that half smile that always tickled her insides. "Okay, let's get this done then. I'm ready for a shower and some really greasy hamburgers and fries."

"Gross." But really, Cambri couldn't agree more.

Twangy country music blared through large speakers in the small, crowded room. Cambri glanced around, noting how it hadn't changed at all. Same barn-style walls, same wooden floor, and same ugly florescent lights. The only difference was it seemed more crowded than she remembered. Even at 5:30, the place was already packed. A quick look around brought her back to high school and how she'd let Jace coerce her into coming here way too often.

"Wow," said Cambri. "Either the food is better than it used to be, or the band must be a popular one."

Jace murmured something unintelligible as he focused on something behind Cambri. She turned around to see a familiar looking woman with long, blond hair headed their way. Her hand was being held by a curly-haired guy trailing behind.

When she caught up, her smile brightened. "Jace, what a surprise to see you here." The guy moved to her side, still holding her hand.

"Hey, Jace, how's it going?" he said.

Several more people walked in the door, crowding the space. Jace pulled Cambri in front of him and rested his hands on her shoulders, sending shivers down her spine. "Cambri, this is Eden and Drew, some really good friends of mine. They live in Bridger as well and were married a few months ago. You might already know Eden. She was a sophomore when we were seniors."

No wonder she looked familiar. "Oh, that's right." She nodded at Eden then glanced at Drew. "But you're not from Bridger, are you?"

He shook his head. "Jace and I met in college."

"Oh," said Cambri. "Is that how you two met? Did he introduce you?"

An awkward silence descended, making Cambri wonder what she'd said.

Jace finally chuckled. "That's one way of putting it."

Another awkward pause.

"What's another way?" Cambri asked, more than a little curious.

"I was dating Eden when Drew came to town and stole her away from me."

"Oh." Open mouth, insert foot. Cambri cringed, not liking the thought of Jace dating someone else, talking to someone else, getting emotionally involved with someone else. Had he once been her best friend as well? "I'm so sorry. I didn't mean to bring up—"

"It's okay," Jace cut her off. "Everything worked out for the best."

Eden watched Jace with a nervous anticipation. "Really?" she said.

"Really." He sounded so sure, so unaffected by it all. His fingers squeezed Cambri's shoulder, as though assuring her it was true.

Drew put an arm around Eden and hugged her close. "You guys want to join us?" He gestured in the direction they'd come from. "There's plenty of room at our table."

Jace's fingers slid from Cambri's shoulder to her hand, where they interlocked with hers, leaving behind a trail of tingles and goosebumps. Hmm . . . she could get used to this.

"If it's okay, we'll pass for tonight," said Jace. "But definitely some other time, okay?"

"Okay." Drew nodded in understanding, then looked at Cambri. "It's really good to meet you, Cambri."

"You too."

Eden waved goodbye and followed her husband away.

Cambri leaned against Jace's chest and glanced up, breathing in the spicy smell of his cologne. "What was that all about?" she murmured.

A slow smile touched his lips. "Let's just call it restoration."

"I see."

Jace relinquished her fingers and placed his hand on the small of her back, guiding her toward one of the few empty tables left in the room. Cambri purposefully slowed her steps so she could enjoy his touch. It suddenly felt as though their friendship had morphed into something that went a little deeper. She liked it.

She squeezed past a large man in a cowboy hat and slid into a seat.

They ordered their meal and had to raise their voices to be heard above the noise of the ever-increasing crowd. When the food arrived, Cambri picked up a limp sweet potato fry, gave it a shake, and laughed when it bounced.

"Hasn't anyone told you not to play with your food?" Jace stole it from her and ate it. "I can't believe you don't like these."

Cambri dunked one in ketchup and gave it a try. It turned to mush in her mouth, and she grimaced as she swallowed. "And I can't believe you do. It tastes like baby food."

"How do you know what baby food tastes like?" he teased, shoving a few more fries in his mouth.

"Okay, Mr. Semantics. It tastes the way I *imagine* baby food would taste. Happy?"

"Happy."

She picked up her burger and took a large bite. Either she was hungrier than she realized, or it had been too long since she'd had one, because it actually tasted good. Well, decent at least. "Not bad," she said.

Jace grinned. "Congratulations. It only took you ten years to say what your heart's known all along. Whether you like it or not, you're a sucker for good, old-fashioned American food. Admit it."

She leaned across the table and lowered her voice, as though ready to tell him a secret. "Never."

"Killjoy."

Cambri laughed. She'd almost forgotten what it felt like to connect to someone the way she did with Jace. Her mother once told her to marry her best friend, but at the time, Jace wasn't even close to the romantic figure she'd dreamed of marrying. She'd responded with a "Gross!", making her mother laugh.

But then a few years came and went, and her friendship with Jace grew stronger. She'd even found that she liked his arms around her when he gave her a hug and enjoyed his touch when he'd nudge her or lean close to whisper something only she could hear. And when he'd kissed her . . . suddenly the thought of marrying her best friend didn't seem gross at all. That's what scared her the most. As much as she cared about her best friend, she didn't want to be held back. There was too much she wanted to do.

So she'd left to have her experiences, go to school, and get away from temptation. She met new friends, dated a bunch of guys, and eventually realized that friends like Jace were about as common as seeing dragon fruit in the produce section of a local grocery store. Not common at all.

As she finished off her hamburger, she couldn't help but wonder that if she hadn't gone away and experienced a life outside of Bridger, would she have appreciated Jace the way she did now? Would she realize how rare a find he was? Probably not. Sometimes it took going without to make you realize that you'd rather have it with. And Jace was definitely with. She knew that now.

"Want to dance?" he asked.

Cambri eyed him with hesitation. This wasn't a new thing, him asking her to dance, but it had always been to an upbeat song—unlike the slow, romantic melody that now played in the background. What would happen if she danced with him? How much more would her heart break in a few days when she had to leave and say goodbye?

Jace stood and held out his hand to her. "You know we can't leave here until we do. It's tradition."

Could something still be a tradition even after years of it not happening? Cambri placed her hand tentatively in his, and he pulled her to her feet. Then he linked his fingers through hers and led her to the middle of the room where a few couples were already dancing in a small, circular area devoid of tables, including Drew and Eden. They smiled and nodded.

Jace pulled Cambri close, holding one of her hands in his and resting the other at her waist. It was old-school, as though he'd been taught by his grandfather, and Cambri loved it. That was Jace, the way he'd always been, standing apart from everyone else and doing things his own way. It showed in his house, the way he interacted with people, and in the way he danced.

Cambri caved to the temptation to lean her head against his shoulder and close her eyes. His arm tightened around her, pressing her closer, and she was lost to the daydream of what it would feel like to be held by Jace every day, to wake up to him every morning, and snuggle beside him every night. To work together and play together and eat greasy hamburgers behind her father's back.

Could she really get on the plane on Tuesday and leave this all behind? Her heart hurt just thinking about it.

Cambri burrowed closer, forcing her mind to a happier place. A place where they fixed up that house together and planted a new maple tree—one that would grow large enough to hold a tire swing for cute little dark-haired, dark-eyed children that would look just like—

"Cambri?" his voice whispered into her ear.

"Hmm?"

"The music's stopped," he whispered again.

"I don't care." Why did he keep interrupting? Cambri wanted to stay lost in her happy little dream of what could be.

He chuckled and took a small step back, moving his shoulder away from her head. "The band's taking a break. No one's dancing anymore."

"What?" Jolted back to reality, Cambri looked around, noting that she and Jace were the only people still on the dance floor. Most people didn't seem to pay attention, but a few knowing smiles came her way, including Eden's.

Jace looked down at her and grinned. "You were falling asleep, weren't you?"

"No, I was just, uh . . . thinking." *About you . . . and our future kids. And you.* Oh, geez, what had come over her? She took a deep breath to try to clear her muddled thoughts as Jace led her back to the table, where he relinquished her hand. It suddenly felt so lonely.

"I think I should probably get you home. You've had a long week."

What? Home? But it was only seven o'clock! Cambri frowned, nowhere near ready to say goodnight. "No, really Jace. I'm not tired at all. I was just thinking."

"About what?"

Cambri's fingers drummed against the counter as she searched for a reason that didn't include future little Jaces and Cambris swinging from a tire swing in the front yard of *his* house. "About your, uh . . ." *C'mon, Cambri, think, think, think.* "Store." It was the first thing that came to mind and something she'd been wondering about anyway.

Jake shot her a half skeptical, half confused look. "You were thinking about my store? Why?"

She forced her fingers to stop drumming. "You never talk about it, but at that zoning meeting, you made it sound like . . . I don't know. Is everything okay?" She eyed him nervously, wondering if she had any right to ask.

Jace drew his brows together, as though trying to switch his train of thought to something completely off-topic. "Yeah, it's okay. Not great, but okay."

"What's going on?" With the music no longer playing, at least Cambri didn't have to raise her voice to be heard.

He glanced around as though not sure if he really wanted to get into this right now, then gave a sigh of resignation and leaned forward, resting both elbows on the table. "When Grandpa retired, my parents took over for a few years while I was away at school. They overspent and made some unwise supply purchases that they weren't able to sell or return. On top of that they didn't keep accurate records, which resulted in a large IRS fine that I'm still trying to pay off. It doesn't help that business is slower than it's ever been."

"Oh no." Cambri suddenly felt even worse for purchasing her plants in Ft. Collins. She should have gone through Jace, even if it meant putting in a special order and waiting for them to arrive. "You're not going to have to close the store, are you?" *Please say no.* After all he'd sacrificed to keep it going, that was the last thing he'd want.

"No, it's not as bad as that. At least not yet. It'll just take longer to pay down the debts, which means I can't reinvest or make updates anytime soon. It's kind of at a stand-still, but if things continue to go the way they have been, then we might be in trouble." He fiddled with his napkin. "New homeowners tend to frequent hardware stores, and that small influx of increased business would have been helpful, that's all. But really, we're fine. "

He didn't look nearly as confident as he sounded, which tore at Cambri's heart. She placed her hand over his, stopping him from massacring the napkin. "Is the developer still interested? I could help you put together a campaign to convince everyone—"

"I've already tried, Cam," he said, cutting her off. "You and I both know how stubborn and resistant to change most people are, and it would just be a waste of time and money."

He was probably right. Still, she hated the thought of giving up. "Is there anything I can do?"

"From North Carolina?" He chuckled. "I seriously doubt it. But thanks for asking."

No, from here, was on the tip of her tongue to say, but she swallowed the words. "I told you before that I could recommend some plants. What about increasing the size of your nursery? Plants aren't too costly, and with it being spring, now's the time to start stocking up." He should have started a month earlier, but better late than never.

He nodded slowly, cautiously, as though trying to think of a way to let her down easy. "It's a good idea and all, but I don't know. That aspect of the business is the one I know least about—or any of my staff, for that matter. I'm not exactly comfortable ordering a bunch of inventory when I don't know what it is or how to go about selling it."

"And like I told *you* before—I can help."

He lifted a skeptical eyebrow. "How?"

Cambri squeezed his hand. "I'll make you a list tomorrow, including the descriptions about each plant, and you can put the order in on Monday. If you or your customers have any questions, I'm just a phone call away."

Jace turned his hand palm side up and closed his fingers around hers, caressing her knuckles with his thumb. "What if I don't have any questions? Can I still call?"

Cambri's heart started to race. "I'd love it if you did."

Something crackled in the space between them, warming her heart and the air around them. Cambri didn't dare blink for fear of breaking the connection.

Ask me to stay. Or at least tell me you don't want me to go.

If he did, Cambri wouldn't get on that plane on Tuesday. Simple as that.

The deep voice of the lead singer sounded, announcing the next song, which turned out to be another slow one. Jace remained quiet, still rubbing her knuckles with his thumb.

Fine, if you're not going to ask me to stay, at least ask me to dance. Her eyes pled with him. When the silence continued, she grew impatient, anxious to be back in his arms. "Want to dance again?"

One corner of Jace's mouth lifted. "I don't know. Are you going to fall asleep on me again?"

And just like that, the spell was broken. Cambri frowned. "I already told you. I didn't fall asleep."

"Yeah. You were thinking about my store."

"Right." Sort of.

Jace chuckled as he pushed his chair back and tugged lightly on her hand to get her to follow. Once on the floor, he pulled her close, and she immediately snuggled against him. Song after song, fast or slow, they danced that way, oblivious to the people around them. Cambri breathed in his scent, soaked up his warmth, and wondered how she'd ever get on that plane Tuesday morning.

When the band finally called it quits, she reluctantly let him go. Jace drove her home, walked her to her door, and wrapped her into a cozy bear hug. "I'm going to miss you, Cam," he said quietly.

Cambri's heart broke a little at his words. Was he okay with her going? Was she the only one having a problem with it? "I'll miss you, too."

He pulled back and looked into her eyes. "Yeah?"

"Yeah."

Ever so slowly, he lowered his head, resting his forehead lightly against hers. His breath was warm and minty.

Intoxicating. "If I kiss you right now, will it be another six years before you come back?"

Her heart thundered in her chest, ready to break free. "I might never leave if you do." There, she'd said it. Her deepest desire was now out there for him to take or leave.

His lips curled slightly before he lowered his mouth to hers. Although it was a slow and cautious kiss, Cambri felt every touch, every sensation. Her hands found their way to the back of his neck, and she tugged him closer, wanting him to tighten his hold and kiss her harder. Instead, his body stiffened, his lips left hers, and he pulled her back into a hug, resting his chin on the top of her head.

"I was thinking we should hold off building the shed on Monday," he said.

Cambri smiled against his chest. Was that his way of saying he wanted her to stay?

"We've been so busy with the yard that your dad hasn't gotten much time with you this past week, then I went and selfishly stole you away tonight. So I was thinking I could get the shed up next weekend, and you can spend your last two days with your dad instead of working."

It was Cambri's turn to stiffen. Ever so slowly, she placed her palm against his chest and pushed back, pulling free from his embrace. He didn't want her to stay after all. He didn't even want to spend Monday with her like they'd planned.

He grabbed her hands and gave them a squeeze. "I'm going to miss you, Cam," he said quietly. "Don't be a stranger."

He was letting her go. The kiss hadn't been a plea for her to stay, it had been a goodbye. For Jace, this was just one night—a brief walk down memory lane, complete with a bonus lesson on how to say goodbye the right way.

Whatever it was, it was over.

When tears pooled at the back of her eyes, Cambri pulled free. "Miss you too," she managed to say, before fleeing inside and hiding behind the large wooden door. With her back pressed against it and the shadows of the foyer hiding her, she listened to his engine rumble away and let the tears fall.

Jace drove away with a sick feeling in the pit of his stomach, like he'd just let something really important slip through the cracks. He shouldn't have kissed her, shouldn't have reminded himself what it felt like to touch her. It had taken every ounce of willpower not to crush her to him and let her know exactly how much he cared and how much he didn't want her to go.

As much as it hurt to say goodbye, it was Jace's only choice. Maybe if they stayed friends, if they kept in touch, if he visited her in Charlotte and she came back to Bridger once in a while . . . maybe she'd eventually decide to stay for good. Or maybe Jace would decide to sell the family business and find something to do in Charlotte.

Either way, at least now there was a chance.

Unlike the last time he'd kissed her goodbye.

Ten

On Sunday, Cambri went through the motions of caring for her dad and keeping him company. She even played chess and backgammon with him, thinking that it would help get her mind off Jace and the depressing prospect of returning to Charlotte. But when her father declared check mate fifteen minutes into the game and grumbled about her worthlessness as an opponent, Cambri pulled out her laptop and researched plants for Jace's store. If she couldn't stop thinking about him, she might as well follow through on her promise to make him a new order list. Once that was finished, she started on the design for his yard. It came so easy, probably because she'd always known what she wanted to do with it, and somewhere around midnight, she printed out a small-scale drawing and paper-clipped it to the list of plants. Then she set it aside.

On Monday morning, Cambri took a utility knife to one of the large cardboard boxes containing her father's new shed. She wasn't about to leave it for Jace to do on Saturday, like he'd suggested. When he showed up ready to work, he'd find the shed all done and get a new order list and the plans for his yard instead.

Cambri grabbed the sheaf of instructions, read the first few steps, and dropped to her knees to start locating the right screws and parts. It didn't take long, and soon she was screwing together what would become the base of the shed.

Her father appeared from around the corner, holding her cell phone. "Where's Jace?" he asked. "I thought he was coming today."

"He had other work to do," Cambri lied.

"You can't do this by yourself."

"Watch me." She eyed the phone in his hand and lifted an eyebrow. "Expecting a call on my phone, or were you trying to check up on me?"

He held it out to her with a frown. "It won't shut up," he said gruffly. "Whoever keeps calling must have something important to say."

Cambri took it from him and peered at the display. Ten missed calls. Hope flared for a moment, then died when she saw they were all from Dillon, not Jace. She shoved the disappointment aside and returned the call.

"Finally," Dillon said without preamble. "Where have you been?"

"Outside."

"Aren't you packing? You're still scheduled on the first flight out tomorrow, right?"

"Right."

"Good." His voice sounded incredibly chipper for ten o'clock on a Monday morning Charlotte time. "You're never going to guess who just called."

"Who?"

"Remember that privately funded museum project we bid on last summer? The one we wrote off because they ended up choosing another company?"

"Yeah."

"Turns out that other company went belly-up before they could get started, and since we're the second choice, they now want us."

Cambri pressed the phone closer to her ear. "Are you kidding me?" The museum project included over an acre of manicured gardens, walking trails and fountains. They planned to hire artists to sculpt boxwoods and create motifs in the sidewalk. Cambri and her team had spent weeks drawing up plans and working on their presentation. She'd put her heart and soul into it, and when they chose another company who'd come in with a lower bid, she'd been devastated.

But now they wanted their plan after all. She could hardly believe it.

"This is your pet project," said Dillon. "I want you to head it up."

"Me?" Cambri had never overseen a project of this size, and the thought of being the one to make all the final decisions was unnerving. Was she even ready? Could she do it?

Yes. Yes, she could. It felt like an answer to a prayer and was exactly what she needed at the moment. The perfect distraction. "When do I start?

"The timing couldn't be more perfect," Dillon said. "You can dive right in when you get back tomorrow."

"Sounds terrific. See you then."

The line went dead, and Cambri stared at the phone, willing herself to feel the excitement she would have felt only a month before. This was the kind of design most landscape architects could only dream of doing. Her name would even be engraved on a plaque located in the center of the garden, listing her as one of the creators. And it was hers for the taking.

Why, then, did she feel so devoid of emotion, so empty?

"When do you start what?" her father's voice cut through her thoughts, and Cambri realized he'd been standing there the entire time, listening to her side of the conversation.

"Oh. A new project. An amazing new project."

"You're still planning on leaving?" He sounded surprised, as though he had no idea she was booked on a flight the next morning.

"You know I'm leaving tomorrow, Dad."

"I know you have a plane ticket, but I didn't know you were leaving." He looked at her as though she'd lost her marbles. "What about Jace?"

Her fingers tightened around the phone. "What about him?"

"I thought you two . . . well, you know."

"You thought wrong." Just like Cambri had. Thought wrong, hoped wrong, dreamed wrong.

Her father rolled his eyes as though she was acting like a drama queen. "Stop being such a cinderblock. Any fool can see the way you feel about him. Why do you keep running away when it's obvious you belong here with him?"

Cambri was not in the mood for this conversation. "Because it's not obvious, Dad. I've worked hard, and I'm good at what I do. And because of that, I've just been offered the project of a lifetime. Why can't you just be happy for me?"

"How can I be happy when you're making the wrong choice?"

"But that's just it, it's *my* choice to make, not yours," she said, jabbing her thumb against her chest to emphasize her point.

"Of course it is," he said. "Just like going to Pennsylvania for college was your choice and taking that job on the other side of the country. I'm not trying to force you to stay. Just telling you you're a cinderblock if you don't."

"Well I happen to like cinderblocks!" It was the dumbest comeback ever, but Cambri didn't care.

"Of course you do. If you didn't, you wouldn't like yourself much, now would you?"

"Stop it!" Cambri redirected her finger at him. If he was the kind of father she could turn to or talk to, maybe then he'd understand exactly why she was getting on that plane in the morning. But he didn't, and he wouldn't understand even if she tried to explain. "You don't know what you're talking about or what I'm thinking or what Jace is thinking or what anyone is thinking for that matter. If you did, you'd know that Jace *wants* me to get on that plane tomorrow."

"Bullwinkle. That has to be the stupidest thing I've ever heard you say."

Cambri clenched her fists and glared. "Good thing I'm leaving so you don't have to put up with my stupidness any longer."

A spark of humor glinted in his old eyes. "That's not a word."

"Neither is bullwinkle!"

"Sure it is. It's the name of that stupid, cartoon moose."

Cambri suddenly wanted to throw something at him but kicked the cardboard box instead. Then she sent her father a scathing glare and stormed away—or, at least started to until she remembered the shed. She stopped and turned, pointing a finger at the house. "Actually, you go. I need to finish this."

Her father shrugged. "Okay, but if you need any cinderblocks, you know where to find them."

Her finger jabbed harder toward the house. "Now!"

"Okay, okay." He held up his hands in surrender. "Just don't blame me if you go back to your hoity-toity job in North Carolina and figure out you're missing something more important than that *amazing* new project."

Cambri clenched her jaw and jabbed one last time.

He finally took the hint and left.

As soon as he was gone, Cambri grabbed one of the flaps and yanked hard, tearing the box open and scattering metal pieces everywhere. She'd finish the shed today, then tomorrow she'd get on that plane and leave Bridger behind without a backward glance. Thanks to her father, she almost looked forward to it now.

Almost.

Eleven

Cambri shivered in the chilly night air as she struggled to hang the shed door on its hinges. At one point, her father had come out carrying a sandwich—a peace offering, he'd called it—which Cambri had accepted, knowing that was as good of an apology as she'd ever get from him. He picked up the instructions, looked them over, and together, they spent the remainder of the afternoon working on the shed. He located the parts and told her what to do, and she did the work, with occasional help from him. While she was grateful for the help, she was even more grateful that he didn't make any references to either Jace or cinderblocks. When his breathing became labored, Cambri had sent him inside.

As she'd watched him go, a peaceful feeling settled in her heart. At least this time she and her dad would part on peaceful terms. And maybe, just maybe, they'd eventually have that normal father-daughter relationship she'd always craved.

Now it was close to ten o'clock. Cambri was alone, thoroughly sick of the shed, and cold. As she twisted the last screw in place, a car pulled in the driveway, blinding Cambri with its headlights. She squinted into them, trying to figure out who it could be. They flicked off, and Lydia's face appeared in the moonlight.

"Hey, you." Cambri straightened and smiled, walking over to give her a hug. "I'm so glad you dropped by. I kept meaning to call, but time got away from me."

Lydia waved her off. "No worries. Jace told me how busy you two have been. That's how I found out you're leaving tomorrow."

A dull ache registered in Cambri's stomach. "I really wish we could have had that dinner."

"Me too." Lydia shivered and rubbed her palms together. "You about done here? It's cold."

"Just finished." Cambri took a step back to admire her and her father's handiwork. "What do you think?"

"That it looks like a prefabricated shed. But a nice one."

Cambri laughed. "You're right. But it's my prefabricated shed, so I'm pretty proud of it."

Lydia grabbed her by the arm. "My car's warm. Let's go for a drive. That is, if you can spare an hour or so."

"Definitely."

As Lydia pulled away from the house and drove slowly down the street, she said, "I envy you."

Cambri shot her a look of surprise. "Me? Why?" Who in their right mind would envy her?

"You had the nerve to go out on your own. I bet you've had so many adventures." Her voice sounded wistful, even sad.

It was a good reminder for Cambri. "You're right, I have. And it has definitely been an adventure. I think it took leaving for me to learn who I am and what I want out of life." Too bad she was a slow learner, and the things she realized she wanted were no longer within her reach *because* she'd left.

Forcing sad thoughts from her mind, Cambri studied her friend's beautiful profile. Lydia had always been kind of shy and reserved on the outside, but fun and witty underneath. It made Cambri wonder how many people were missing out because they didn't know her friend. "Why haven't you ever left? You sound like you'd like to." It would probably be really good for Lydia if she did.

Lydia laughed and waved her hand in a dismissal motion. "Are you kidding me? I don't have your guts—or anything close to your guts. I wish I did. I'd give anything to have an adventure, and maybe even a fling." Her eyes widened, like she'd just said something shocking, making Cambri laugh. And think.

An idea sparked, and Cambri twisted in her seat. "Your wish is my command."

"What?" Lydia shot her a confused glance.

"You're off for the summer, right?"

"Yeah."

"Come visit me in Charlotte," said Cambri. "I can give you a list of sights to see during the day, and we can hang out in the evenings after I get off work. On the weekends, we can drive to the most beautiful beaches you've ever seen or take a road trip to DC. What do you say?" Having Lydia come to stay might be exactly what Cambri needed to distract her from thoughts of Jace. On the other hand, it could be a bad reminder too, but none of that really mattered. What mattered was that Lydia wanted an adventure, and Cambri was just the girl who could give her one.

Provided she said yes.

Lydia had drawn her bottom lip into her mouth and was worrying it back and forth.

"Unless you have other plans for the summer," said Cambri.

"No, of course I don't. It's just that . . . well, I've never even been on a plane before." There was hesitation in her voice, as though she was embarrassed to admit it.

"Well, now's your chance to see what it's like."

Silence, more worrying of her lower lip, and finally Lydia smacked the wheel with her hand. "You know what? You're right. I'm in. I'm going to buy a plane ticket, visit you in Charlotte and have the summer of my life."

"Don't forget the fling. I happen to know a cute guy or two I could set you up with," Cambri teased.

Even in the darkness of the car, Lydia's blush showed. "Oh, I was only kidding about that. I mean, who needs a fling when there are *so* many guys in Bridger to date?"

"As in . . . ?" Cambri prodded.

"Oh, you know. Sam, the grocery bagger. Jimmy at the repair shop. He's cute. And—oh, a couple of my students have single fathers who are just dying to date me, so there's that too."

Cambri giggled, loving the release it gave her body. Even if Lydia was a constant reminder of Jace, they would still have the time of their lives. Lydia was that much fun to be around.

She returned her attention to the window and immediately tensed, the smile slipping from her face. Lydia had just turned down Rose Street. Why? Her friend's smile had vanished too, and she was back to worrying her lower lip in a guilty way, as though she was doing something she shouldn't be doing.

"Where are we going?"

Lydia cleared her throat. "I thought we'd stop off at Jace's place so you could say goodbye before you left."

"We've already said our goodbyes." The closer they got to Jace's house, the faster Cambri's heart raced. Why was Lydia doing this to her?

"Yeah, a lousy goodbye, at least according to Jace," said Lydia. "I'm pretty sure he wants a do-over."

"Pretty sure?" No way would Cambri get out of the car with only a *pretty sure*.

Lydia pulled into the driveway and stopped, turning a sympathetic smile on her friend. "Ever since you two started working on your dad's yard together, Jace has been happier than he's been in a really long time. But today when I talked to him, I've never seen him more miserable." She paused. "Go talk to him, please? He's been through a lot this past year, and I hate seeing him like this. I can't believe that either of you want to leave things like this."

It was Cambri's turn to chew on her lower lip. Lydia was right. She didn't want to fly back to Charlotte feeling this way, but did she have the courage to knock on his door and try to change that? To tell him point blank that she was willing to stay if he wanted her to? Her heart pounded, and her fingers clutched the armrests, not moving.

"You're the brave one, remember?" Lydia said quietly.

No. Cambri wasn't brave at all. She was a runner. A fleer. A person practiced in the art of avoidance maneuvers. And what she wanted to do right now was jump out of the car and run straight to the airport.

So pathetic.

But maybe it was time to grow up a little and start facing things head on, like an adult.

I can do this.

Still, her hands continued to clutch the armrests.

Jace's front door opened, and he appeared, squinting through the darkness. Cambri wanted to duck and hide, but a gentle squeeze from Lydia's cold fingers made her reconsider. She drew in a breath and yanked the handle, then stepped from the car. As soon as the door closed, Lydia's car backed away.

Cambri glared at the person she thought was her friend. "Traitor," she muttered.

Not knowing what else to do, she clasped her hands together and walked slowly toward Jace. When she got within talking distance, she stopped. "This was all your sister's doing."

"I figured."

Now that they'd got that out of the way, what now? Cambri shuffled her feet, feeling both awkward and cold.

"Want to come inside?"

She hesitated. Did she, or would this turn into another lousy goodbye?

You're the brave one, remember? Lydia's quiet voice echoed in her mind.

"Okay," Cambri finally answered.

They walked inside and stared at a room that was still a work-in-progress. There was no couch or loveseat—nowhere other than a cluttered kitchen table or bar stool to sit.

Cambri sighed. "You'd probably be done with this room by now if it weren't for me."

"I doubt it," said Jace. "The store keeps me pretty busy, and I don't exactly have money coming out my ears, so I have to wait and do projects as I can afford them." He gestured toward the stairs, and Cambri sat down, then scooted over to make room for Jace. His shoulder brushed hers, sending warm tingles down her arms.

"I'm glad Lydia coerced you into dropping by," said Jace.

"Tricked me is more like it."

A small smile touched his lips. "She can be sneaky like that. But I'm still glad she did. Even though we already said goodbye, it felt . . . unfinished. And I don't know why. I mean, you're leaving tomorrow and there's nothing I can do to change that. So what else is there but to say goodbye and hope we keep in touch?"

"You can ask me to stay," Cambri's voice was so quiet, she wasn't sure he'd heard.

He leaned forward and rested his elbows on his knees, his dark gaze piercing hers. "No, I can't. I don't want to hold you back, Cam. You cut me out of your life before, when you thought I was trying to keep you here, and I'm not about to give you a reason to do that again. If returning to Charlotte is what you want, I'm not going to stand in your way no matter how much I want to."

He wanted her to stay. Cambri's heart suddenly felt lighter and less broken. "You don't have to stand in my way to keep me from getting on that plane. I just needed to know that you wanted to."

Jace shifted positions, and their knees touched as he faced her. "I do want to. I want to build a blockade, slash the plane's tires, and disconnect the fuel line. But this has to be your choice."

"It is." Cambri met his gaze, ready to lay all her cards on the table. "I've regretted walking away from you since the day it happened. Even though I've had other relationships, you've always been at the back of my mind—the dream guy I let slip away." She lifted a finger to his chin and ran it across his five o'clock scruff. "If you're offering me another chance to see what could be, I'm taking it. I—"

Jace closed the distance between them and kissed her the way she'd wanted him to kiss her Saturday night. His lips moved over hers in a hungry, searching way, and Cambri responded with the same. They were suddenly back in that old Mustang, only this time Cambri had no reservations—no reason to pull back or run away. This time, she knew what she wanted.

Her fingers cupped the back of his neck, pulling him closer and closer still, until a pain registered in her back and shoulders, marring the moment. *Stupid hardwood stairs.* She shifted slightly, trying to make the pain subside, but it only intensified, and she finally had to push him back. "Sorry, but my back is killing me."

"I can fix that." Jace stood and pulled her into his arms. He kissed her again, only slower and more carefully, taking his time. He kissed her until Cambri's senses were reeling and she couldn't catch her breath. Only then did he finally back away, dropping his forehead against hers.

"Remind me to thank Lydia for tricking you."

Cambri snuggled against him. "I know. Who would have thought she had it in her? She's always so sweet and—" Cambri jerked her head up, nearly smacking Jace in the face. "Oh, no. Lydia! I invited her to Charlotte with me for the summer. I promised her an adventure and a fling."

"A fling?" Jace raise an eyebrow. "You promised her a fling?"

"How can I do that if I'm not going to be there?" Her eyes pled with him to tell her what to do. "We've already made plans, and you should have seen the look of excitement on her face. I can't disappoint her now." Cambri frowned, feeling one of her happy little bubbles burst. "Maybe I should go back, at least until the end of the summer. My condo's lease isn't up until then anyway. I could finish up one last project at work and—"

Jace's finger rested against her lips, shushing her. "Do you *want* to go back?"

"No."

"Good, because I don't want you to either, especially if you're going to search out guys for summer flings."

"Fling, not *flings*," Cambri corrected.

Jace linked his fingers behind her back and nudged her closer. "Lydia's a big girl. If your condo is available, I don't see why she can't go on her own. In fact, I think it would be really good for her."

"I agree. But that's the point. I don't think she'll go if I'm not there."

"Oh, she will," said Jace with that adorable half smile she loved. "We'll make sure of it."

"And how will we do that?"

"By using the same method she used tonight. Trickery. We'll pack her bags, kidnap her, then drop her off at the airport with no ride home. It will be like a mother bird pushing her baby out of its nest."

He had a point. Still, Cambri worried about sending sweet and inexperienced Lydia into the heart of Charlotte, with all its noise, traffic lights, and confusing street names. How would she handle it?

"I don't know," Cambri said slowly. "I need to make sure she's okay with it first."

"Just leave the talking to me." Jace's thumb traced over Cambri's lower lip, sending goose bumps scurrying up her arms. "But now, I'm through talking about my sister."

Cambri's laugh was muffled when his lips covered hers, effectively removing all thoughts of Lydia and Charlotte and summer flings.

Twelve

Bridger, Next Left

Cambri smiled at the faded green and lopsided sign. After five long days in a car, it was a welcome sight. The overcast sky threatened rain and gloom, but Cambri didn't feel gloomy at all. The deep green of pine trees and Kentucky blue grass appeared more vibrant and lush against the gray-hued skies, and a feeling of rightness stirred in her chest. She was home. Really home.

How much had changed in only three short weeks.

Cambri glanced at Jace, asleep in the passenger seat, and smiled. His lips were parted slightly, and quiet snores sounded in the car. He'd driven most of the day, but by late afternoon, he'd finally given in and let Cambri finish the drive home.

He'd insisted on flying to Charlotte to help her pack and move her stuff back because he didn't want her driving cross country alone. The apartment was furnished so there wasn't much to pack, and with Lydia coming in June, Cambri made sure to leave a few pans, dishes, and utensils behind. Like Jace had promised, he'd been able to convince her to still go, not that it took too much convincing. She'd even teased, "It will be much easier to have a fling without Cambri there, getting in the way."

They'd all laughed, and Cambri had helped Lydia buy her first airline ticket.

Since Jace insisted on having an adventure as well, they'd turned "the move" into a week-long road trip. They spent a day at Cape Hatteras beach, drove out of their way so Jace could take in the sights of history-rich Washington DC, then hit a few additional places on their trek home, like the Mammoth Cave National Park in Kentucky. Every day seemed to lessen the time they'd spent apart, and soon it felt like she'd never really left. Cambri wondered how she'd lived without him in her life for so long.

As much fun as the past week had been, Cambri was ready to sleep in her own bed, implement the plans she'd been working on for Jace's house, and get started on her new landscape design business she planned to run out of the Sutton Hardware Store. According to Cal, who'd filled in for Jace while they were gone, a bunch of unfamiliar plants had arrived on a flatbed and were selling like hotcakes. Everyone in town was oohing and ahhing over "all them new and pretty plants."

Cambri, who'd listened in on the conversation with her ear pressed to Jace's, had shot him an I-told-you-so look. He'd tweaked her nose in response.

Now here they were, ready to leap into a new life together.

Cambri pulled to a stop in front of her father's house and poked Jace in the ribs. "Wake up, sleepyhead," she said in a sing-song voice.

He gave a short snort, making Cambri laugh, and she poked him again. "Don't make me have to kiss you awake."

His lips twitched slightly, letting Cambri know he was awake, but his eyes remained closed.

"Okay, you asked for it." Cambri unbuckled her seatbelt and leaned toward him. "But I think it's only fair to warn you that I just ate the last of the sour cream and onion chips."

One dark brown eye popped open. "Rain check?"

"Not on your life." She leaned the rest of the way and planted a full kiss on his lips. Then she blew into his face and laughed when he puckered.

She slugged him in the arm. "Stop it. I was only kidding about the chips. My breath doesn't smell that bad, does it?"

"No." He gave her a peck on the lips to prove his point. No matter how many times he did that, it never got old.

She cocked her head at him and smiled. "Did you know that you snore?"

He frowned. "Do not."

"Do too. You sounded like an angry warthog making a huge fuss over—well, nothing."

"Liar, liar, pants on fire."

"Next time I'm going to record it on my phone, and then you'll see."

A slow smile spread across his face. "Will there be a next time?"

"Sure, we can do it right now." Cambri nodded toward the house. "Go challenge Dad to a game of chess, and you'll be back asleep in no time."

"You're right. That should do the trick." Jace flopped his head against the back of the headrest and glanced at the house. "Remind me to have a pre-nup drawn up with a clause stating that I will never have to play chess with that man. Fishing, I can handle. Chess, not so much. It's like . . ."

Jace continued to talk as though he'd said nothing out of the ordinary, but Cambri's racing heart said otherwise. He'd just said pre-nup, right? Had she heard wrong? Jace finally stopped talking and looked at her, his eyebrow quirked up. "Something wrong?" he asked.

"You said pre-nup."

Jace lifted an eyebrow, as though he had no idea why she was making a bid deal out of it. "So?"

"Pre-nup, Jace!" Cambri said. "That's not something you toss out in the middle of a conversation about chess. Especially when you're not engaged or planning—"

"Not engaged *yet.*"

Cambri gaped at him, feeling a little stunned. Most couples approached this subject with a little more subtlety and warning, didn't they? What did that mean anyway? Was Jace popping the question, or just telling her he was *planning* to pop it?

"Cat got your tongue?" he teased.

She gaped at him, then shook her head to clear her thoughts. "When, exactly, are you thinking of getting engaged?" A little warning would be nice, unlike this conversation.

Jace leaned forward and gave her mouth another peck. "That's for me to know and you to find out, but I really hope you'll say yes when it happens." He reached for the handle. "C'mon. Let's go check on your dad and get some dinner. I'm starved." Then he was out of the car, acting as though nothing out of the ordinary had just happened.

Cambri, on the other hand, sat frozen.

Jace was planning to propose. To her.

The house, the dark-haired, dark-eyed children, Jace—it could all be hers.

She stared out the window, feeling like she'd just stumbled upon a meadow filled with the most beautiful wildflowers imaginable. The overcast sky became rich with sunlight. Warmth and happiness rushed around her, dancing across her skin. She'd never felt so alive, so complete, so—

"Coming?" Jace had walked around and opened her door, and now held out his hand. Cambri looked up at his handsome face with his endearing, lopsided smile. She didn't deserve him.

"Earth to Cambri," Jace said, breaking through her thoughts. His fingers wiggled, inviting her to take them, which she did. He pulled her from the car and kept her hand securely in his as they walked toward the house, where her father waited on the front porch in his favorite rocker.

"About time you got out of that car. You'd think after being in it all day, you couldn't wait to get out."

Jace smiled at Cambri. "We were just . . . making plans."

"What did you do, propose?" said her father.

"I wouldn't dare without asking your permission first."

Harvey shook his head at Jace as though he were a dimwit. "Boy, if you don't already know what my answer will be, you're about as smart as a bag of rocks."

Jace chuckled. "I'll take that as a yes."

Harvey leaned back in the rocker and looked at Cambri. "Get things worked out with your former boss?"

"Not *quite* former, just yet," she said. "He's not happy with my decision—or with me, for that matter—but I know a lot about this project, so he still wants me involved. It will mean a bunch of conference calls and maybe a few visits out there in the fall, but I think I can manage."

Her father harrumphed in response.

Cambri leaned against a pillar and looked over the yard that she'd spent so many hours recreating for her father. A few weeds had sprung up in her absence, but other than that, it was the same, filled with young and budding life. Or, at least almost the same.

She squinted at the far corner of the lawn, seeing small orange flowers that weren't there before. She rose and walked to them. Someone had dug a too-deep hole and shoved in three marigold starts next to each other. It was the work of rough and unpracticed hands. Her father's hands.

Marigolds had been her mother's favorite flowers because they reminded her of sun on a beautiful summer's day. Every year she'd planted three. One for Cambri, one for her father, and one for herself—just like her father had done here. Cambri swallowed the lump in her throat as tears stung her eyes.

"Guess I should have planted one more for Jace," came Harvey's voice from behind. Cambri spun around and threw her arms around her dad. He tensed at first, but then relaxed and hugged her back.

"Thank you for remembering," she said.

He cleared his throat, but Cambri could hear the raw emotion. "I've never forgotten," he said. "I tried to, but then you had to go and show me that I was wrong, and I hate being wrong." He moved to the side, but kept an arm around his daughter as he looked over all the changes Cambri had made. "When we first moved in, there was grass everywhere, and your mother made me dig up all those flowerbeds. Then she planted and planted and planted. I kept getting after her to stop spending so much money on frou frou, but she just smiled and told me I'd be glad when it was all done. And she was right. She made this house a home. I didn't realize how much until I'd gone and messed it all up." His voice dropped to a whisper. "Thanks for bringing her back to me."

Cambri swiped at the tears spilling down her cheeks. Happy tears—the kind you get when someone reaches into your heart and touches it with a gentle and loving hand. Although her father would always be rough around the edges, underneath all that roughness was someone worth loving and someone who loved her.

Cambri looked up and caught Jace watching from the front porch with his shoulder leaning against the post and his eyes focused on her. She smiled, wiping at a few remaining tears.

Some might say that the world was filled with imperfect people, and because of that, perfect moments didn't exist. But Cambri knew better. This moment proved it, though it wasn't easy to come by. It took leaving, coming home, lowering her pride, and learning to find the good. It took heartache, loneliness, tears, and sorrys, as well as forgiveness, acceptance, love, and a whole lot of growing up.

And looking back, Cambri wouldn't change a thing. All that hard stuff had turned her into a stronger, wiser, and better person than she was before—someone who realized that she had something worth having. And that something was pretty great.

Continue on for a sneak peak of Book 4 (Lydia's story) in the Ripple Effect Series.

Author's Note

Dear Reader,

I'm so grateful to you for taking time out of your day to read *Righting a Wrong*. I hope that it gave you a much-needed break from the craziness we call life.

If you can spare the time, I can't tell you how much I'd appreciate a review on Amazon, Goodreads or wherever else you feel inclined to leave one. Word of mouth is the best kind of advertising there is, and we could use your help getting the word out about this series.

If you enjoyed this book and would like read about my other books or get notified of new releases, you can find me on the web at RachaelReneeAnderson.com.

Thanks again and happy reading!
Rachael

Acknowledgements

To Karey and Kaylee, my co-collaborators in this project. You are both brilliant writers, wonderful editors, and good friends. I hope this is the beginning of a lot more fun projects to come.

To Donna K. Weaver, Julie N. Ford, and Jennifer Griffith—you guys rock! The stories you imagined and wrote are so unique and fun. Thank you for putting your trust in us and for being so great to work with.

And to my family, for being the wonderful, supportive people you are. Especially my husband, Jeff. I thank Heavenly Father every day for your presence in my life.

About Rachael Anderson

A *USA Today* bestselling author, Rachael Anderson is the mother of four and is pretty good at breaking up fights, or at least sending guilty parties to their rooms. She can't sing, doesn't dance, and despises tragedies. But she recently figured out how yeast works and can now make homemade bread, which she is really good at eating.

You can find Rachael online on Facebook, Twitter, or at RachaelReneeAnderson.com.

Coming next in the Ripple Effect Romance Series
(Available April 21, 2014)

Lydia was supposed to have an adventurous and exciting summer. Instead she's done nothing more than read and eat takeout. Now it's time to go home, and what does she have to show for it? A big fat nothing. Unless, of course, her trip to the airport somehow turns into something more than just a flight home.

Blake feels like he's been sent on a wild goose chase. While work is piling up back in Denver, he's on the other side of the country, hunting for some mysterious box that his grandfather left him. Well, no more. Nothing inside that box could possibly be more important than the opportunity to make it as the youngest partner at his firm. So he's going home, and that's that. But that's before he discovers his flight has been cancelled.

When these two strangers meet at the airport, they make a split-second decision to search for the box together. Maybe with both of them on the hunt, Lydia can have her adventure and Blake can find the box. And maybe, if they're lucky, they'll even find some romance.

One

Lydia lifted her bag onto the scale and crossed her fingers it would meet the weight restrictions.

"Either you're a mighty fine packer or you're right lucky," said the man behind the counter. "Forty-nine pounds for one and forty-nine and a half pounds for this one." His thick, mahogany mustache moved as he spoke and reminded Lydia of a squirrel's tail.

"I guess I'm a little of both. I weighed them on a bathroom scale, but you never know how accurate they are. The scale said they'd be three pounds under."

"Now you know your scale weighs light. Probably didn't want to know that, did you?" He laughed at his little joke and Lydia tried not to stare at the rodent on his upper lip. "You need to go to Gate C-14. Glad you gave yourself some time. That gate's quite a jaunt from here."

Squirrel Man pointed to his right. "Go past the restaurants and stores, and you'll find the C concourse on your right. It's just past The Traveler's Friend. Now that's a piece'a irony, calling it a traveler's friend. I can buy a gallon of O.J. for what they're chargin' for a Dixie cup." He held his fingers up to demonstrate the tininess. Does that sound like a friend to you?"

Lydia laughed. "No, sir. It doesn't."

"You have a nice flight, Miss Sutton."

Lydia headed in the direction Squirrel Man had pointed. She'd taken only a few steps when the wheels of her carryon malfunctioned and the bag flipped onto its front side—the side without wheels—again. "This is the last trip I'm taking with you," she muttered to her suitcase. Of course, considering this summer, maybe she'd never take a trip again.

After Lydia made it through security, she stopped at a little deli and bought a sandwich before continuing to her gate. Squirrel Man had been right. The walk to C-14 was long, made even longer by the cheap wheels of her carryon.

Lydia felt clammy and uncomfortable. The air conditioning in North Carolina's humid heat was a ninety-pound weakling fighting a steroid-swollen heavyweight champion. The C concourse had to be at least the length of a football field. Up ahead was C-14—just past the mob of people waiting at C-12 for a flight to Miami.

Lydia maneuvered her way through the throng. "I'm so sorry," she said after her suitcase flopped over and upended an older gentleman's bag. Finally, the crowd thinned and she was at her gate, next to a few scattered early birds who sat in the powder-blue, vinyl chairs. Eyeing the seats facing the window, she cut through two rows. As she turned the corner, her suitcase flipped again and snagged on a chair leg, upsetting her balance. Her purse slipped down her arm to the crook of her elbow. Lydia wrenched the suitcase back to its wheels and kept moving. The purse, now dangling from her elbow, caught on the armrest of a chair, yanking her to a stop. Her Sensational Sandwich sack flew out of her hand

and landed on the floor a few feet away.

Lydia took a deep, cleansing breath, unhooked the purse strap from the armrest, righted the carryon, and looked for her wayward sandwich.

"Is this what you're looking for?" asked a handsome man.

Perfect. Of course Lydia's sandwich acrobatics would have to be witnessed by a guy who looked like a movie star. And not a Nick-Nolte-mugshot movie star, either. This guy was more like a Ryan-Gosling-freshly-shaved-and-in-a-perfectly-tailored-navy-suit-with-a-super-crisp-white-shirt movie star.

"Thank you," she said and took her sandwich before dropping into the closest chair. Forget looking out the window. It wasn't worth the effort. Lydia blew the hair out of her eyes and dragged her bag closer to her feet.

"You doing okay?" the Ryan Gosling lookalike asked from across the aisle. Laughter was barely contained behind his very nice smile. Lydia sighed and shrugged her shoulders.

"I am now."

The man turned his attention back to his laptop, but his smile lasted several more seconds. Lydia pulled her turkey on wheat sandwich from the crumpled bag. She hadn't eaten since breakfast and that had been a sad little spread. Earlier in the week, Lydia had packed up Cambri's few remaining belongings and shipped them to Colorado. Yesterday, she had completely cleaned out the apartment, including the few condiments that were left in the refrigerator. She didn't want to lose her deposit because of a half bottle of ketchup and an expired jar of relish. This morning, the only thing left to eat had been a browning banana and the last few swallows of milk.

When Lydia took the second bite of her sandwich, a tablespoon-sized glob of mayonnaise oozed out the bottom and into her hand. She fumbled one-handed through the bag in search of a napkin. Was this a joke? The only thing left in the bag was a mayonnaise packet. Didn't need that. "I can watch your bag while you go wash up." It was the handsome man, and his mirth had reached beyond his fantastic smile (he had a perfect dimple that appeared by the right corner of his mouth) and up to his twinkling blue eyes. Lydia looked from the man to her fistful of mayonnaise. A robotic female voice in Lydia's mind recited lines about leaving bags unattended and not accepting packages from strangers. "I promise I won't take it and make a run for it," he said.

"You'd be terribly disappointed if you did," Lydia said, making up her mind. She returned the rest of her sandwich to the paper bag, pulled her purse onto her shoulder with her condimentless hand, and headed for the restroom, holding her mayonnaise like a gift in front of her. "I'll hurry."

When Lydia approached her seat a few minutes later, an airport security officer with a shiny face and a little paunch was standing in the aisle by her suitcase.

"Is this your bag?" he asked.

"Yes. Is everything okay?" Why hadn't she paid attention to the voice in her head?

"It appeared to be left unattended. In the future, I'd advise you to either take your bag with you or move it closer to your boyfriend when you leave."

Lydia shot a surprised glance at the movie star, and he shrugged. "Sorry, babe. I told him you'd be right back, and I offered to move your bag over by me, but he wanted me to wait for you to come back."

Lydia almost choked. She knew he was just rescuing her from the security guard, but no one had ever, ever called Lydia "babe" before and certainly no one as handsome as Ryan Gosling. It had a wonderful ring to it. Was her racing heart because of being questioned by an officer of the law or because this man had just called her "babe?"

Lydia dragged her distracted gaze back to the much less

interesting man standing by her bag. "I'm so sorry. I just had to make a little run to the ladies' room. It won't happen again."

"See that it doesn't. Airport security is no laughing matter." Was she laughing? "Have a nice flight."

Lydia sat down by her bag. "You should probably move over here by me since you're my girlfriend. We don't want to make him suspicious."

"Oh. Of course. I should have thought of that." Did the movie star want Lydia to sit by him? Lydia rolled her eyes at her silliness. He was just trying to keep from being hassled any further. He went back to working on his laptop as she moved her things across the aisle. "Sorry about that," Lydia whispered.

"No problem." He looked up from his computer and smiled. Oh. My. Wow! Up close his dimple was even cuter. The bigger the smile, the deeper the dimple. "Are you taking a trip to Denver?" he asked.

"What?" She dragged her eyes away from his mouth. "Oh. I'm headed home."

"You're from Denver?"

"Just north. I live in Bridger."

"I live in downtown Denver," he said. "I'm Blake, by the way."

"I'm Lydia."

"What brought you to North Carolina?"

Lydia shook her head and sighed. Telling the truth about her summer in Charlotte was humiliating and disappointing. Of course, she could make something up, but that was the cowardly thing to do and this summer was supposed to have been about being brave and adventurous.

"You can't say?" he asked when she didn't answer. "Was it some top secret mission you can't talk about?" He sat up a little straighter and closed his laptop.

Lydia tried not to stare at his mischievous eyes as she

thought about how to answer. A little piece of bravery with this stranger wouldn't salvage her failed summer, but at least she could finish with a tiny victory. She took a deep breath. "I was supposed to have a summer full of adventure and new experiences, but unfortunately, I learned I'm not very adventurous." Blake looked confused, so Lydia explained. "My friend loaned me her condo for the summer. Her instructions were to 'go somewhere new every day. Meet new people. Do adventurous things.' I'm afraid I failed."

"Come on, I'm sure you did something adventurous," Blake said.

Lydia shook her head. "Nothing." She reached down and unzipped the pocket of her suitcase. "Unless you call sitting on a lounge chair on the roof of the condo with a book an adventure." She pulled out three books and held them up one at a time. "Look at these. Quest for Parts Unknown is about this guy searching for the remains of an expedition to the North Pole forty years ago. They never returned, so he was trying to discover what happened to them. He got caught in a terrible storm and barely made it back alive. From Sea to Shining Sea. This woman lost her job and broke up with her boyfriend, so she decided since she had nothing tying her down, she'd walk from the tip of Florida to the top corner of Washington, relying only on the kindness of strangers. It took her almost five months, but she did it."

Lydia started to hold up up the third book then blushed. "I read about other people's adventures," she said as she moved to tuck the books back into her bag, "but I didn't have any of my own."

"Come on. I don't get to see that last book?" Blake asked.

Lydia was caught. Without looking at him, she handed Blake the book. The cover was embarrassing. A male model with perfectly floppy hair had his hands over the eyes of a female model in a "Guess who?" kind of pose. It was brightly backlit and the title was written in a romantic, flowing script. The woman at the bookstore had gushed about it and Lydia hadn't wanted to hurt her feelings, so ten minutes and $12 later, it left the store in Lydia's bag. "Love at Tenth Sight? What's this one about?" Blake didn't even try to stifle his laugh, and Lydia's blush deepened.

"It's about a woman who's given up on love because she's had her heart broken so many times and, finally, she meets her soul mate."

"Had she actually had her heart broken nine times?"

Lydia wished she'd left that book in her bag."Well, I haven't finished it, but yeah, I guess so."

"You spent your summer reading these?"

"These and about a dozen others," Lydia admitted.

Blake whistled. "Sounds relaxing, but you're right. Not very adventurous."

Lydia shoved the books in her bag. "I wasted an entire summer, and now I get to go back and report that I'm dull and unadventurous."

"You have to give a report?"

"That was the deal. Free condo in exchange for a full report of my summer exploits."

Lydia wanted to kick herself. This had been a once in a lifetime chance to do whatever she wanted. School was out, so she'd had no students to look after and no principal to report to. With Jace and Cambri checking in on Grandpa, nothing had stood between Lydia and three months of excitement.

On her first day in town, she'd stopped at a trendy hotel and picked up brochures about kite-surfing and a bike tour through civil war battlegrounds. She'd thought about backpacking into Great Smoky Mountains National Park and camping overnight by herself. That would have been adventurous and even a little rebellious because she knew her mother would totally disapprove. Lydia had even scouted out a singles mix-and-mingle at a local bookstore and speed dating at a nice restaurant not far from the condo.

But Lydia hadn't done any of it.

"I did try Indian food," she said, shaking her head. "I wanted to have something exciting to tell my students when we did the 'what did you do this summer' assignment so they'd think I was a cool teacher. Somehow, I don't think they'll be impressed that I ate curry."

"You teach school?"

"I teach fifth grade at Juniper Heights Elementary. It's in Fort Collins." Blake's face looked sympathetic, and Lydia hated how pitiful she sounded.

"Don't feel too bad," Blake said. "I'm headed home as a failure, too." Lydia lifted an eyebrow. "I just wasted three days I couldn't afford to lose on a wild goose chase. Now I'm headed home with nothing to show for it."

"What kind of goose chase?" Lydia asked. "Unless you can't tell me because it's classified."

Blake showed his dimple. "My grandfather made me promise I'd go find a woman named Gladys. She's had a box of his things for more than fifty years, and I was supposed to get it."

"More than fifty years?" Lydia asked. "She probably doesn't even have it anymore."

"That's what I thought. But Grandpa called her last year, and she still has it. He told her he had a grandson who needed to see what was in the box, and she said to send him to North Carolina for it. Except I can't find her. She doesn't live at the address he gave me, and the woman that lives there now has no idea where she is."

"Why do you need to see it?"

"I don't know. He said when I saw it, I'd understand."

"So you're leaving with nothing?"

"Oh no, I've got something. I've got $800 in wasted air

fare and a stack of paperwork even deeper than when I left."

"I'm sorry," Lydia said.

"It wouldn't be a big deal, but I'm so close to making partner, and I don't want anyone to think I've lost my focus."

"Partner where?"

"Collins, Strider and Van Wagoner."

"I'm sure you'll be fine. Just tell them you worked while you were away," Lydia said, pointing at his laptop.

"And you can tell your friend you ate Indian food." They laughed.

Blake put his laptop in his briefcase while he spoke. "The worst part is that I was really curious about what Grandpa wanted me to have."

"Can't he just tell you what it was?"

Blake shook his head. "He died in April." He leaned forward, his elbows on his knees, fingers clasped in front of him, and stared absently across the wide concourse.

"I'm sorry." Instinctively, Lydia put her hand on his arm. Horrified, she snatched it back. What was she doing touching this man? He was a handsome stranger, and she was an unadventurous schoolteacher whose only human interactions over the past three months had been with the clerk at the bookstore and the takeout deliverymen. She had no business touching him.

Blake turned his head toward her and smiled. Lydia felt short of breath and hoped he couldn't tell that her jackhammer heart was trying to demolish her ribs and escape her chest.

"Thanks, Lydia. I should have come as soon as he told me about it, but things at the office were busy and I didn't want to look like I was making something more important than the firm. I guess I figured I had time."

"Will you try to find her another time?"

"I don't know. I have a letter he wanted me to read after I'd gone through everything in the box. That might tell me something, but it feels wrong to read it without doing what he asked. It's like I'm cheating him."

"Attention passengers."

The voice sounded like Mrs. Jackson, Lydia's sophomore history teacher. Mrs. Jackson had recited the same test questions for forty years and sounded like a recording that had been slowed down to half speed. "Who was an American mechanical engineer who used scientific management to improve industrial efficiency in the early twentieth century?" By the time she'd read the question, the class was nearly asleep.

"Flight 1758 from Charlotte to Denver has been delayed by thirty minutes. Again, flight one seven five eight from Charlotte to Denver has been delayed by thirty minutes. We apologize for any inconvenience. Please see the counter if you have any questions or if you have connecting flights in Denver. Thank you."

Blake and Lydia looked at each other and laughed. "Wow. Glad she got that out before the thirty minute delay was over," Blake said. "I guess I have time to go get myself a sandwich."

"I'll watch your bags," Lydia said with a smile. She was surprised when Blake slid his briefcase and duffle bag a little closer to her feet.

"I should probably tell them to go light on the mayo, right?" he said.

"Good idea. And be sure they give you some napkins."

Instinctively, Lydia started to pull out her book, but not wanting to be caught reading Love at Tenth Sight when Blake returned, she changed her mind and watched two children playing Uno on the floor.

"I hope you like brownies," Blake said when he returned ten minutes later.

"I love brownies."

"Good. I was afraid you might tell me you were allergic

to chocolate."

"Sometimes I wish that were true. Thank you. That was thoughtful of you."

Blake ate his sandwich, and Lydia took a bite of the brownie. "Mmm. This is good. Would you like some of it?"

"Thanks. I've got one for myself in the bag," he said.

"Attention passengers." Thankfully it was a new voice, and this one spoke at a normal speed.

"Uh oh," Blake said.

"Due to mechanical difficulties, flight 1758 from Charlotte to Denver has been cancelled. Please bring your tickets to the counter to reschedule. Again, flight One Seven Five Eight, from Charlotte to Denver, has been cancelled. Please bring your tickets to the counter to reschedule your flight."

The world came alive around them. Snatches of conversations could be heard as people gathered their belongings.

"They'd better be giving us a free flight for this."

"And how about some food vouchers. I'm starving."

"I'd rather they cancel the flight than send us off in a faulty airplane."

"I'm going to miss my connecting flight."

"Well, that's not very convenient," Lydia said. "At least I have something to read."

Blake laughed. "I think they have to make arrangements for us to get on a flight right away, even if it's with another airline."

Blake and Lydia stayed in their seats as the area around them cleared and a line formed. Finally, Blake stood, picked up his duffel bag and briefcase, then waited while Lydia gathered her things. They took a spot at the back of the line. After a minute, Lydia spoke.

"Since you have to change your flight anyway, maybe you should stay another day or two and try to find the box."

The corner of Blake's mouth twitched. "Maybe you should stay a couple of days and have an adventure."

"Touché. I guess if the plane had gone down, I'd have had an adventure to tell about. Or not tell about."

The line moved slowly. "You know," Blake said. "Maybe your adventure could be staying and helping me find my grandfather's box."

Lydia nearly choked on her last bite of brownie. Was he joking? They didn't even know each other.

"I have to be back for teacher's meetings. And I need to get my classroom ready for school to start. The desks are all stacked up in a corner of the room and I need to get them set up and organized and I've got to put up a couple of bulletin boards. And I have to get papers for the parents copied for back to school night and . . ." Blake's smile widened as she spoke. "And I'm babbling, aren't I?"

"Yeah. Don't worry about it. I should get back to the office anyway. It was a crazy idea."

"Yeah," Lydia said, relieved. A few minutes passed, and they neared the front of the line. A voice in Lydia's head wouldn't be quiet. You're a coward. You don't really want an adventure. You're all talk. You could kill two birds with one stone. Have an adventure and help this guy find the box from his grandfather. But you're too big of a wimp. She wanted to tell the voice to mind its own business, but it wouldn't shut up. Chicken. Scaredy cat. But this wasn't about adventure. This was about good, common sense, right? It wouldn't be smart to stay with this man she didn't know. And yet her instincts told her this guy was safe, that she didn't need to fear his intentions.

It seemed the only way to stop the nag in her head was to speak. "It wasn't a crazy idea. It was an adventurous idea. And I came here for adventure. I need something to tell Cambri when I get home, right? And you need to find that box or you'll miss out on something important. And I don't technically have to be back until Wednesday morning, so…"

"Really? Are you just talking a big game?" Blake teased.

"You're not a psychopathic killer, are you?"

"No. But I certainly wouldn't tell you if I was."

"That's true. That would really up the whole adventure factor, though."

"See, you're braver than you thought."

"Do you really want to do this?" Lydia asked, not sure what she wanted his answer to be.

"I don't know if I'll make it back here any time soon, and it would be nice to feel like I gave it an extra effort."

"Maybe this cancelled flight is a sign. But I really do have to be at work Wednesday morning."

"So do I. If we fly home Tuesday, that gives us two days to find Gladys."

"Oh help," Lydia whispered, and Blake laughed, showing his dimple. That was all it took. When they reached the front of the line, Blake and Lydia changed their flights to the 8:10 departing flight on Tuesday evening.

If you enjoyed this chapter and would like to read more, *Lost and Found* can be found at:

Amazon.com